HIDEOUS KINKY

HIDEOUS KINKY

by
ESTHER FREUD

HARCOURT BRACE JOVANOVICH, PUBLISHERS
New York   San Diego   London

Requests for permission to make copies of any part of the work should
be mailed to: Permissions, Harcourt Brace Jovanovich, Publishers,
8th Floor Orlando, Florida 32887.

Frontispiece by Lucien Freud.

Library of Congress Cataloging-in-Publication Data
Freud, Esther.
Hideous kinky/by Esther Freud.—1st ed.
p.   cm.
ISBN 0-15-140216-7
I. Title.
PR6056.R47H53   1992
823' .914—dc20   91-47673

First published in 1992 by Hamish Hamilton, Ltd.

Printed in the United States of America

First edition

A B C D E

For my mother and my father

CHAPTER ONE

It wasn't until we were halfway through France that we noticed Maretta wasn't talking. She sat very still in the back of the van and watched us all with bright eyes.

I crawled across the mattress to her. 'Maretta will you tell us a story?'

Maretta sighed and turned her head away.

John was doing the driving. He was driving fast with one hand on the wheel. John was Maretta's husband. He had brought her along at the last minute only because, I heard him tell my mother, she wasn't well.

Bea glared at me.

'Maretta ...' I began again dutifully, but Maretta placed her light white hand on the top of my head and held it there until my skull began to creep and I scrambled out from under it.

'You didn't ask her properly,' Bea hissed. 'You didn't say please.'

'Well, you ask her.'

'It's not me who wants the story, is it?'

'But you said to ask. I was asking for you.'

'Shhh.' Our mother leaned over from the front seat. 'You'll wake Danny. Come and sit with me and I'll read you both a story.'

I looked hopefully at Bea. 'Oh all right,' she relented, and we jumped over Danny's sleeping body and clambered up between the two front seats.

' "Will you walk a little faster?" said a whiting to a snail. "There's a porpoise close behind us, and he's treading on my tail." '

I sat warm against her and joined in when she got to 'Will you, won't you, will you, won't you, will you join the dance?' 'Will you, won't you, will you, won't you, will you join the dance?' until we heard the rustle of Danny's sleeping-bag as he sat up in the back.

'D'you want me to take over soon?' he yawned.

John kept his eyes on the road. 'Half an hour.'

Danny was my special friend. The first time we'd met he'd magicked a sweet, a white sugared almond, out of a pipe for me. I had been waiting ever since for a good opportunity to ask him to do it again. Now he was always either driving or sleeping. Or Bea was there. Bea was two years older than me and there were some things you had to keep secret about. Anyway, I thought, however magic Danny said these almonds were, they'd be bound to run out like any others.

That evening we stopped to cook. My mother made soup with carrots and potatoes in a metal pot on a camping stove. We sat on the grass verge and ate.

'Maretta?' My mother held out a bowl to her.

Maretta looked at the ground.

'Maretta would you like some soup?'

She turned her face away.

My mother's hand began to tremble. It made the spoon rattle on the tin side of the bowl as she stretched it out to her.

We waited.

'Well, all the more for us,' she said finally, pouring the soup back into the pot. Her voice was high and tight. Maretta smiled serenely.

A truck roared by. A wave of hot and cold laughter

2

swept over me and I bit my lip and stirred my spoon noisily.

John stood in front of my mother, between her and Maretta. 'She'll be all right once we get to Marrakech. She'll be all right.' He put his arm around my mother's waist. 'I was married to her for four years. I should know.'

She let her head rest limply on his shoulder. 'I still think we should take her back.'

They stood by the side of the road rocking gently from side to side.

'Danny?' I felt this might be my lucky moment. 'Will you magic me a sweet?'

Bea, who was sitting nearer than I thought, raised her arched eyebrows. I screwed up my face in warning.

'Damn and blast.' Danny slapped his hand on his knee. 'I've gone and forgotten my pipe.' He lowered his voice and said with a laugh, 'Well maybe we should go back to London after all.' And he squeezed my disappointed face between his fingers.

Late the following afternoon we arrived at Algeciras and drove the van on to the ferry. We got out and stood on deck. Bea and I leant against the railings and waved enthusiastically at the straggle of Spaniards on the quay. The air was thick with the smell of fish and oil. Some men in blue overalls waved back. Almost before we lost sight of Spain, Morocco began to appear at the other end of the boat. A long flat shadow across the water.

'Land ahoy!' Bea shouted out over the sea. 'Land ahoy!'

We ran fast from one end of the boat to the other waving goodbye to Spain and shouting 'Land ahoy!' to Morocco. The sun was sinking fast and the gulls had stopped circling. As we leant over the railings, Morocco faded into the night and we could only guess at the layers of blackness where the sea stopped and the land began. We went back to the van. Maretta was sitting in the front seat.

3

'Where are the others?' I asked, climbing in, forgetting for a minute.

She didn't answer. Bea stood by the door.

'Come on. Let's go and find them.'

'Would you like to come?' I touched Maretta's hair. It was thick and damp with dirt.

Bea pulled my arm. 'I'll race you to the deck.'

Maretta didn't move. Not even her eyes.

'All right then,' I said, and I started after her on a hopeless challenge.

The ship was lit now by the white froth of the waves. We edged along where earlier we had run. At the front of the boat we heard laughter and snatches of familiar voices. We crept forward, our eyes on the red tips of cigarettes.

'Land ahoy!' Bea jumped out of the darkness and put her hands over my mother's eyes. She screamed with mock alarm.

'Your money or your life.'

Mum put her hands in the air and pleaded for mercy. 'I don't have any money,' she said. And everybody laughed.

A slow, low hoot rose into the air and we all jumped. Danny picked me up and swung me over his shoulder. 'Right. Back to the van,' he said.

I called to Bea as I hung, the blood rushing to my head, 'I'll race you,' and I drummed my hands on Danny's back to make him go faster.

We sat in the dark in a queue of cars waiting for our turn to drive off the ferry. My mother showed us our photographs under hers in a black leather passport.

'In a minute a man will come to check that it's really us,' she said, tucking my hair behind my ears. John was in the driving seat, and Danny and Maretta were awake in the back. The line moved slowly forward car by car.

'Once we're through customs it should only take a couple of hours along the coast road and we'll be in

4

Tangier,' Danny said. He talked with a rolled cigarette unlit and hanging between his lips. 'I just wish they'd get on with it.'

We were edging now towards a white barrier. Two men in uniform inspected each car before the barrier lifted into the sky and let them through.

There was a tapping on the glass. We sat very still and John rolled down the window, letting in a blast of cold and salty air and a whiskery face with bright blue eyes. 'Hi, where you heading?' he said, sticking his head right in and peering at us in the semi-darkness.

'Tangier tonight . . . and then on to Marrakech.'

'Hey, I'm heading that way myself. Dave. Call me Dave.' And he rested his elbows in the open window and smiled.

Dave ambled along beside us as we neared the barrier. 'So this is your first trip, you'll love it, you won't want to leave. Where you from? Let me guess? London. Forget London, man. Marrakech. That's where it's at.' He had a scarf tied round his head and his pale ginger hair hung over it in strands. He had no bag and no coat. 'Hey brother,' he slapped John on the shoulder, 'you're going to need some introductions. I'll tell you what. I'll ride into Tangier with you. What do you say?' And he whipped open the van door and leapt in.

Dave settled himself in the back.

'Hey lady, how you doing?' he grinned at Maretta.

She didn't answer.

Another face appeared at the window. A dark, serious face with a thick moustache. My mother leant over and handed him our stack of passports. He flicked through them and glanced at us each in turn. A quick flick of a glance and he handed them back. The customs man nodded towards Dave who was hovering on a mound of cushions by the back doors. He said something I didn't understand. John and my mother both shook their heads

5

but Dave stuck out his long white neck and nodded. The officer was silent for a moment and then he jerked his thumb backwards. He was telling the van to turn around. Back, round, and on to the boat. Back towards Spain.

The barrier stayed firmly closed.

We ate our breakfast in Algeciras. Bread rolls and Fanta. Maretta sipped a cup of black coffee and forgot to wipe away the marks it left on either side of her mouth. Mum said it was lucky they hadn't stamped 'undesirables' in our passports. She said if we saw Dave or anyone who looked like Dave at the barrier at Tangier we mustn't talk to him.

'Is it very hideous to be an undesirable?' Bea asked. Hideous was Bea's and my favourite word. 'Hideous' and 'Kinky'. They were the only words we could remember Maretta ever having said.

'Hideous kinky. Hideous kinky,' I chanted to myself.

'It is ... if you want to get into Morocco,' Mum answered.

When we arrived in Tangier later that day after a short and sunny second crossing there was no Dave in sight. The officers waved us through with only a glance at our passports and everyone except Maretta shouted and yelled as loud as they could to celebrate.

CHAPTER TWO

We were still hours away from Marrakech when the van backfired, veered sharply off the road into a field, and shuddered to a halt. John got out and opened up the bonnet. He stood for a long time peering in at the engine with his hands in his pockets and a knowing, not-to-be-disturbed look on his face. 'Actually, I haven't a clue what I'm doing,' he said eventually, and he and Mum began to giggle.

Bea was worried. 'We can't stay here for ever,' she said. The field stretched as far as I could see. There was nothing much in it, just grass and a lot of flowers. Poppies and daisies.

'No we can't stay here for ever,' I repeated, because it was always safest to be on Bea's side. We both got back into the van and waited for Mum and John to stop laughing.

Maretta lay on her side with her arm over her face and her eyes closed. You could tell she wasn't asleep. First she stopped talking, I thought to myself. Then she stopped eating, and now she is never going to move again. Maretta still had the coffee stains from two days ago around her mouth.

Danny had only wanted to go as far as Tangier. We had dropped him off outside a café with an orange and white striped canopy. Danny said goodbye to everyone and then, just as he was leaving, he bent down and tweaked my nose. 'My God, how did that get there?' he said, and a large pebble-white sweet lay in the palm of my hand.

'Do you think they sell sweets in Morocco?' I asked Maretta.

She didn't answer, and Bea said she didn't know.

We sat on the side of the road and watched John grow smaller and smaller as he went off in search of someone who knew something about cars.

Mum stretched out in the grass. 'Tell us a story,' she said.

Bea lay down next to her. 'Go on, tell us a story.'

So I told them about how on the day before we left London I heard two birds talking. I told them all the things the birds had talked about. Breadcrumbs. Other birds. The weather. I told them about the argument they had had over a worm.

'That's stupid, no one understands bird language,' Bea said.

My eyes stung. 'I do.' But my voice didn't sound very convincing.

'Liar.'

I flushed. How could I be lying if I remembered every single word? The more I thought about it the more I wasn't sure. 'Mum ...?'

But she had fallen asleep in the sun.

We followed John into the tiled café. It was set back from the road and was not so far from where our van was now parked.

'It's a French hotel,' John whispered. 'I think it might be a bit expensive.'

'We'll just have some tea,' Mum reassured him, and we sat down in the shade of the terrace.

The tea they brought was made from mint leaves and

8

was very, very sweet. Mum looked into the pot. 'It's like syrup in there,' she said.

John had returned with three Moroccan boys in cloaks with pointed hoods. They helped us push the van along the road to the hotel. Maretta refused to get out. The Moroccan boys didn't seem to mind at all. They smiled and waved at her through the windows in the back door.

We stayed at the café all day while John squinted dismally into the engine. 'I suppose it's a miracle it got us this far,' he said when it began to grow dark.

Mum dragged blankets out on to the road. She made an open-air bed for us in the hotel garden. It was nice to go to sleep on ground that wasn't rushing away from under you.

'I'll have to use those insurance stamps to have us towed into Marrakech,' John said from the other side of Mum.

'Insurance? You?' Mum's astonished voice came back. And Bea asked, 'What's "towed"?'

We sat in the truck, even Maretta, and watched our van dangling along behind us on a rope with John at the wheel. At first Maretta hadn't wanted to move, so John had picked her up and put her in the truck himself. He picked her up easily like a child and she didn't struggle or even move. Now she sat in the front with the Arab man who was driving and who had looked for a long time at the insurance which John said was like money but was really just a lot of bits of paper.

I kept wondering how we'd get home again now that our van had to be dragged everywhere. I thought it might be easier if we could take a boat straight to London. Then I must have fallen asleep. I dreamt about John and Maretta and their little girl who had stayed behind in England, waving to us from a gangplank. We were on a ship and everyone was throwing rolls of toilet paper to

9

their friends on land but we didn't have any toilet paper to throw.

When I woke up I was sitting on Mum's lap in a tiny white room. Mum was talking in French to a small, plump man who smiled when he spoke and clapped his hands together and laughed at the end of every sentence. Bea looked out of a window through which bright white sunlight was falling. The van was parked opposite. It looked tired and dusty. A small crowd of children and flies were beginning to gather.

Akari the Estate Agent, whose shop we were in, poured mint tea into glasses. He poured it from a great height without spilling a drop and then, when the glasses were full, he tipped the tea back into the pot and poured it out again in as high and perfect an arc as before. The tea that was finally allowed to settle was thick and yellow like the eye of a cat.

'Ask him if I can leave the van here,' John said, 'just until I can sell it or get it going again.'

Akari nodded and smiled in response to the translation.

'He says he has a house we can rent in the Mellah. He'll take us round to see it now.'

Akari was already locking up his little shop.

The Mellah was the Jewish quarter of the city. Our house was plain and whitewashed with three bedrooms upstairs and a kitchen and sitting-room below. There was a yard with flowers pushing up between the paving-stones. Maretta walked straight into the house and sat down on the floor. The floors were all tiled with tiles that went halfway up the walls. There was no furniture.

'Akari says we'll need a mijmar,' Mum said, looking round the bare kitchen.

'What's a mijmar?'

'It's a stove for cooking. With charcoal. And we'll need some bellows.'

'I'll get someone to bring the mattresses from the van,' John said, and he disappeared.

'What are bellows?'

'Bea, what are bellows?' But she was out in the garden, kicking at the poppies and the marigolds and searching for salamanders among the loose stones of the wall.

That night, when Mum read to us in the upstairs bedroom, I leant against her and asked, 'Are we there?'

'Yes,' she said, 'we're there. Is it what you thought it would be like?'

I didn't know. I hadn't thought what it would be like.

'How long are we going to stay?' Bea asked.

'Oh I don't know. As long as we want.' She started to read our story to herself. Bea and I waited for her to finish. 'You could go to school here if you wanted,' she added.

'What about me? Couldn't I?'

She stroked the top of my head. 'Maybe in another year or so. When you're as old as Bea.'

I started to sulk, but I was too tired to keep it up. Before I knew it my clothes were being pulled away, up over my head, and I felt the unfamiliar smoothness of a cool, clean sheet catch against my legs.

CHAPTER THREE

After wandering for some time through the lanes of the indoor market, we stopped at a stall that was very much like the others. There were rows and rows of shiny, coloured dresses packed against the walls, and also soft white caftans with thick embroidery round the neck. We stood at the entrance, which was like the mouth of a cave of treasure, and watched as dress after shimmering dress was pulled and shaken and laid on the ground before us. I chose a caftan that looked as if it had been painted. It had blocks of red in it like red liquorice and purple and orange flames. Mum said it made me look a little pale. But if that was what I wanted.

I slipped it over my T-shirt and shorts and felt the slippery nylon swish around my ankles. 'Can I keep it on?'

Mum was busy dressing in a pale purple caftan. It swept the floor and made her look tall and mysterious with her black hair loose and hanging thickly down her back.

Bea chose one in cotton. It had patterns of leaves and stalks and flowers that swirled all over it in blue and green. 'Of course it'll fit,' she said holding it up to her chin.

'Don't you want a shiny one like me and Mum?' I asked, hoping she'd change her mind. But Bea folded up the dress and held it under her arm, so I knew that she'd made her decision.

A cloud of drumming hung above the main square, which Akari the Estate Agent called the Djemaa El Fna. Groups of men moved tirelessly from one spectacle to the next, forming circles to watch the dancers and the tambourine players, the African who dressed as a woman with cymbals on his wrists and a full silver tea-set on his head, the acrobats, and the snake charmers whose songs seeped across the square and mingled with a wailing like a bagpipe I couldn't trace. A waterman roamed from corner to corner clanking his brass cups and calling to the thirsty to buy a drink of his warm and rusty water. I felt cool in my new dress. It was a smart, clean version of what the beggar girls wore, the beggar children who roamed the Djemaa El Fna, chattering and chasing each other, always on the lookout for a tourist to torment. 'Tourist, tourist. Coca-Cola, Coca-Cola,' they chanted in reedy voices as they marched beside their victim, until, unable to endure it a moment longer, the tourist would stop, open up his purse and send the beggar children spinning off, laughing and clutching a shiny new coin. The tourists, having shaken off their entourage, headed for the terraced hotel at the far side of the square. They sat in the shade and ate melon already sliced.

A few days before, Bea and I had slipped up there while Mum was shopping. She was buying dates and oranges to tempt Maretta. We sat at an empty table and fixed our hungry, mournful gaze on a lady with white hair. We watched unblinking as she skewered lump after sliced lump of melon with a silver fork.

But she's only eating half of it, I thought, as the thick and discarded rind piled up. By the time the woman called us over I had convinced myself that I was really starving.

'You win,' she said, giving us each a slice. She spoke with an American accent.

We devoured the fruit right there in front of her, letting the sweet juice run down our arms until there was nothing

13

left but a rind so thin it turned transparent when I held it up to the sun.

'Well, well,' she said, as I placed the rind proudly on the table. I was hopeful of another slice.

Bea pointed out our mother who was wandering between the stalls looking as if she were lost.

'That's our Mum,' I said, forgetting we were meant to be in disguise as Moroccan beggar girls, and we ran out of the hotel to be found.

We chopped vegetables – onions, potatoes, green beans, peppers and tomatoes – on the floor of the tiled kitchen. My mother lit the mijmar and began to cook. The mijmar was a large clay pot that had a fire alight inside it. The tajine was a dish that sat above it with a lid like an upside-down flowerpot, and everything that was going to be cooked had to cook in the tajine, unless it was couscous which could be steamed in a bowl above it.

'Why don't you go up and see if Maretta is eating with us tonight?' Mum said to me when supper was nearly ready. I dragged my feet. We had been in the Mellah for over a week now and Maretta had hardly left her room. I opened the door a crack and looked in. She was lying face down on her mattress, one arm stretched above her head.

'Maretta . . .' I whispered from the doorway. My voice rasped unexpectedly.

'Maretta . . .' I moved towards her. I could tell that she wasn't asleep. She was never asleep. I knelt down by her bed and went to touch her shoulder. Something moved. Something tiny. A grey speck in her hair. I flinched away. Then I saw another. A speck like a grain of dirt alive and moving over her body. Along her neck. Crawling. Crawling. My hands began to twitch as I edged away from her. I shrieked as I clattered downstairs. I ran into the garden and shook myself in a frenzy.

John, who had been rolling a cigarette against the wall, pushed past me and into the house. I heard him running up the stairs and then there was silence. I twitched occasionally and waited.

After a while Bea came out and said in a calm voice, as if she had expected it all along, 'Maretta's got body lice. John is going to take her to the hospital.'

So we stood in the garden and waited for him to bring her out.

John didn't come home that night and my mother gave us both showers standing in a bucket in the kitchen. She heated up a bowl of water and poured it over us with a cup. I flinched at anything that moved. A strand of hair on my neck. Water squelching grey slugs between my toes.

'You don't get lice in England, do you?' I asked as she worked her fingers through my hair.

'Oh, yes,' she said. 'You can get lice anywhere. If you're really dirty they might even follow you right round the world.'

Bea giggled. 'Just waiting to hop on.'

'It's not funny.'

I started abruptly as the sleeve of Mum's caftan brushed my leg. I jolted round in my bucket so fast I almost knocked it over. Mum wrapped me in a towel and lifted me out.

'Where do they come from?'

She hesitated and I could feel Bea listening hard.

'Eggs,' she said. 'They lay eggs. It just takes one lice. Or is it louse? One lousy lice to hop on to you, lay some eggs and then the eggs hatch into lice and then they lay more eggs, and those eggs – '

'Stop it, stop it!' I screamed. I ran upstairs and pulled the covers off my bed and inspected the sheet until I was sure it was all unbroken white. I got in and curled up in the blankets.

When Bea came up I asked her, 'Do you think Maretta is going to die?' and she said, 'I don't know.'

What I really wanted to ask was: 'Can body lice kill you?' and: 'Can they kill you between going to sleep one night and waking up the next morning?'

Two days later I was still twitching every time a blade of grass caught my ankle or a fly whistled past my ear. When, at lunch, the specks of ground black pepper crawling in my soup made me choke on my spoon, Mum had an idea. She packed a bag with towels and soap and shampoo and a tube of Macleans toothpaste.

'Today,' she said, 'we are going to the Hammam.'

The Hammam was a building that was one enormous bath. The walls, floor and ceiling were covered in brick-shaped tiles in blue and green. We stood in a small, warm room streaked with sunlight which slanted from a window high up, almost in the roof, and took off our clothes. A wooden door at the end of the room opened and a woman, wearing just a thick bead necklace, greeted us and held the door for us to go through. A large, damp, steam-clouded room opened on to another, slightly warmer, and another, and another so hot I had to yawn to catch enough breath to breathe.

In the farthest room, which was cooler, there was a cold-water tap and a bucket. As I stood and watched, a woman with overlapping stomachs and hair down to her waist tipped a full bucket of water over the head of a very thin girl who stood with her eyes closed, dark brown and shining. My mother picked up a cake of smooth, soft soap that looked like oatmeal blended with olive-green oil. I followed her back through the hottest rooms into a milder steam, through which I could make out children sleeping stretched out on the floor, and in one corner an old woman rubbing her arms with a grey stone that looked like concrete.

We sat against a wall that dripped with water and blew long breaths. The woman with the necklace appeared, smiling broadly and gesturing with her hand, in which she held a rippled washing stone and a bar of soap. She spoke in Arabic without interrupting her smile.

'Would you like to have a special Hammam wash by this lady?' my mother asked us both, but I couldn't tell from her voice whether she thought it was a good idea or not. I shook my head sideways.

'All right, I will,' Bea said, and I immediately regretted my decision and tried to change the movement of my head without anyone noticing so that I felt dizzy.

Bea stood in the middle of the room. The Hammam woman squatted next to her and rubbed her body with the stone until grains of black dirt stood out all over her.

'Doesn't it hurt?'

She shook her head.

She was splashed clean with water from the cold-water bucket. The Hammam woman lathered soap soft in her hands and, taking each part of Bea's body, rubbed it down as if she were polishing a piece of furniture. Then she took up the bucket, which she poured slowly over Bea's head so that the cold water flattened her hair and the soap ran off her in a frothy river. When the last drip had fallen, she opened her eyes and looked down at her body that glimmered and sparkled in the misty room.

'Is it my turn now?' I said, taking Bea's place, and the lady held my arms and began rubbing them with short swift strokes of the Hammam stone. When my body was so clean it felt like silk, we all washed our teeth under the cold tap, and the Hammam lady and the three small children who had been sleeping in a corner stood and watched.

We were getting ready to go home when my mother opened her purse and took out two coins. 'Bea, go in and give the lady this and say thank you.'

Bea disappeared through the wooden door and returned a few minutes later clutching a brand new stone. 'It's mine.' She waved it triumphantly. 'She gave it to me for a present.'

'How do you know? Maybe it was meant for me.'

'Shh. It can be for all of us.' And Mum pushed the door open on to the noise and dust of the narrow street.

CHAPTER FOUR

Bea and I sat cross-legged on the floor and divided the
beans into two piles. My pile looked bigger than Bea's,
but I decided not to mention it. Mum was crying over the
onions.

'Will John be back in England by now?' I asked, and
she wiped her nose on the back of her hand and said, 'Yes.
I should think so.'

'Did he go back to find Maretta?'

'Yes, I expect so,' she sniffed.

'Why did Maretta go back?' I asked, forgetfully eating
a bean.

'Because the hospital sent her.' I had heard this before,
but I wanted to hear it again.

'Did they send her on an aeroplane?'

'Yes.' She dropped handfuls of onions into the hot oil.

'Did they send John on an aeroplane?'

'No. They didn't send him. He went.'

'Why?'

'Because he wanted to.'

'Didn't we want to?'

'Didn't we want to what?' She stopped and caught my
eye.

'Go home,' I said.

'No. We do not. And please don't eat the beans.'

She stirred the onions angrily as they sizzled in the

tajine. A plate of chopped tomatoes sent the sizzle into a roar and then the stew steamed gently with slowly added aubergine and all of Bea's beans and some of mine.

'When we do go home ...' I asked, 'will it be on an aeroplane too?'

Mum poured olive oil on to the salad and cut thick slices of white bread. 'Let's eat,' she said and she carried the food out into the garden.

It was a warm and light evening and we had gone to the open café in the Djemaa El Fna to eat our supper: bowls of bissara, a soup made with split peas and cumin and a circle of olive oil floating on top. Mum had finished and was talking in French with a man from another table. Bea and I explored the café while playing our own game of tag. The key rule to the game was one invented by Bea to extricate herself in the unlikely event of her ever being caught. As I brushed the edge of her sleeve with my outstretched hand I would have to say something, a word invented by me, but if she saw me coming she could free herself by screaming 'Hideous!' or 'Kinky!' or both a second before I touched her, thereby freeing her to race away between the tables and chairs while I panted behind – running good words over in my head.

It was at the height of this game that a man stopped me as I hurtled past his table. He held on to my arm and looked at me full in the face. I gulped. I was sure I had been swearing. Bea sidled back and stood behind me.

'Why don't you both sit down and take some tea with me?' the man said in perfect English. He stretched out his hand to Bea and introduced himself. 'My name,' he said, 'is Luigi Mancini.' He was tall and thin with pure silver hair that slicked back from his temple to the nape of his neck. 'So you are English,' he smiled. 'What shall I call you? The English Children?'

We told him our names and he leant back in his chair,

drawing on an ivory cigarette holder. He exhaled a gentle line of blue smoke into the air. 'I used to know your father,' he said. 'In London, in the forties, when he wore silver and gold waistcoats.' Luigi Mancini chuckled to himself. 'Does he still wear these waistcoats in silver and gold?'

I wanted to ask whether he meant one silver one and one gold one, on different days. Or whether it was a mixture. One silver-and-gold waistcoat for Sunday best.

'Probably,' Bea said.

I tried to picture my father in London dressed in clothes that sparkled. All that came to mind was a colour illustration from 'Ali Baba and the Forty Thieves'. A man in his forties with pockets full of treasure. I had forgotten that I even had a father.

'I hope you will come and stay with me. I have a house not far from here,' Luigi Mancini was saying. 'With a beautiful garden. Will you visit?'

'Oh, yes,' we both said in unison, and Bea jumped down and ran and found Mum and led her back to the table.

'This is Luigi Mancini. And this is our Mum,' Bea said, and Mum sat down and smiled while a waiter came and poured us all mint tea.

'Can we go?' I asked, when the invitation was presented again, and to my relief she said, 'Of course, we'll go this weekend. If that's all right with you?'

Luigi Mancini waved a hand heavy with rings and said he'd be delighted.

Luigi Mancini was a Prince. There was everything but his crown to prove it. I wandered with Bea through the cool dark rooms of his palace. There were gold-framed mirrors and candles, unlit in every room. I slid over polished wooden floors that creaked between one flying carpet and the next. 'Luigi Mancini, Luigi Mancini,' I hummed as we explored the upstairs corridor.

'Do you think maybe Luigi Mancini will ask Mum to marry him?' I said as we watched them from a bedroom window. They were deep in conversation as they walked in a slow curve around the rose garden. 'Then I could be a Princess and you could be my lady-in-waiting.'

Bea stared out of the window.

'Or if you wanted, you could be a Princess too.'

'Just think, we'd have cornflakes every morning for the rest of our lives,' she said, and we both sighed.

For the last two mornings we'd sat down to breakfast at a table heavy with linen and silver, in the centre of which was a giant box of cornflakes. 'Shipped from England,' Luigi Mancini had said. 'Especially for my girls.'

There was a host of silent servants, all men, who kept the silver shining and the meals flowing and the beds crisp and turned down. They were not the same men who clipped the rose bushes and collected the petals that sat in bowls around the house or mowed the lawn and mended the fences so that the peacocks didn't stray too far.

Luigi Mancini and our mother walked back into sight along a gravel path. He was, as always, dressed in white and Mum looked like a Queen in her purple caftan.

'Anyway, Mum wouldn't want to marry Luigi Mancini and stay in this house for ever and ever.'

'Why not?' I pressed my face against the window-pane to try and lip-read their conversation.

'She wants to have adventures,' Bea said. 'She told me.'

'When?'

Bea didn't answer.

'Will they start very soon?' I persisted.

'Yes, of course.' Bea began to wind herself up in the linen curtain that hung across the window.

'But if she married Luigi Mancini that would be an adventure.'

'No,' her muffled voice came back.

'It would be for me,' I said, trying to unwind her. 'It would be for her if she liked cornflakes.

'Or white bread.

'Or mashed potato.

'Or milk shakes.'

'Or spaghetti hoops,' Bea joined in. 'We could order crates of them and eat them off our fingers like rings.'

'Strawberries,' I said.

'Liquorice allsorts.'

'99s.'

'They'd melt, silly. Wind yourself up in the other curtain and be hidden and we'll see if they come and find us.'

So we stood there, whispering to each other from our separate coils of curtain while we waited in vain for the search to begin.

We walked into the garden to take a final look at the peacocks. 'If there is ever a peacock that doesn't get on with the others and needs a home ...' Bea ventured nervously, 'or if one of the pea-hens has too many chicks, I'd look after it for you. We've got a garden too, you know.'

'Thank you,' Luigi Mancini said. 'That's very kind of you. I'll most certainly remember.'

The car was waiting to take us back to the Mellah. Mum was already sitting inside and, as we approached, the driver started up the engine. Luigi Mancini whispered something to him and strode off without a word of goodbye. The car turned in the drive and Mum looked round at us with a frown.

'What did you say to him?'

'Nothing ... only ...' But before any more trouble was caused the door opened and a fat black hen was thrust on to Bea's lap.

'Sorry she's not a peacock,' Luigi Mancini smiled, but

she'll be very happy with you in your garden. And he kissed his fingers at us as the car pulled away, and called, 'Do come again.'

Bea held her arms tight around the black hen so she couldn't move or flap her wings. 'I'll name her Snowy,' she said. 'Like in Tintin.' I leant over and stroked the top of Snowy's head with one finger. Her round orange eyes darted about like fireflies.

CHAPTER FIVE

If Mum refused to marry Luigi Mancini it was not long before another suitable candidate presented himself.

It was a blue cloudless afternoon and we sat at the front of the crowd in the Djemaa El Fna and watched the Gnaoua dancing. They wore embroidered caps fringed with cowrie shells which tinkled like bells when they moved. They played their tall drums and danced in the square on most afternoons.

'Where do they come from?' I asked Mum.

'They are a Senegalese tribe from West Africa. The King of Morocco has always employed them as his own personal drummers.'

'Because they're so beautiful?' I asked, admiring the elegant wrists and ankles of the dancers as their cymbals rang out in time to the men's drumming hands.

'Maybe.'

Khadija, a plump and solemn-faced beggar girl, wriggled through the crowd and squatted next to me.

'Hello Khadija,' my mother said, noticing her, and Khadija smiled a big gap-toothed grin. She touched my arm and pointed through the crowd across the square to where a group of people were beginning to gather. 'Hadaoui,' she said and began to move towards them, looking over her shoulder to see that I was following.

An old man in faded purple and red robes unfolded a

large carpet on which he placed variously shaped brass pots. He filled each one with plastic flowers. He talked to the people who stopped to watch, spreading ripples of laughter through the gathering crowd. Once the carpet was unravelled and every last ornament was in place it became clear not all his comments were directed towards the crowd, but some to a tall, much younger man, who threw his words back at him quietly and with a half-smile that made the people sway with laughter.

The old man sat in the centre of his carpet and blew into a pipe that twisted around inside a bowl of water and bubbled and smoked with each breath.

'What's he doing?' I looked at Khadija and pointed.

'Kif,' she said, hugging her knees and keeping her eyes fixed on the entertainment.

Bea appeared and sat on the other side of Khadija. 'Where's Mum?'

I looked round to see her standing near the young man who was lifting white doves out of a box and placing them on the carpet. The doves ruffled their wings and strutted about, pleased to be in the open.

'Do you think they're going to do any tricks?'

'Who?' Bea said.

'The doves, of course.'

They didn't. It was the old man who did the tricks. He didn't juggle or dance or swallow flaming swords, but somehow, by talking, mumbling, even praying, he held the crowd, grinning and transfixed, straining for his every word. The younger man seemed sometimes to be his loyal assistant and then, disappearing, would emerge on the side of the crowd, heckling and jibing from amongst them, and, just as tempers began to boil, would disclose himself, much to everyone's delight, by leaping into the open and winking slyly all around. Bea, Khadija and I squatted close to the front, with the hard legs of men pressed against our backs.

26

After the young man had walked twice round the circle on his hands, and the old man had prayed to Allah on a pretend rug, the people seemed to know it was the end. They threw coins on to the carpet and drifted away. I saw my mother throw a coin, but she stayed standing where she was on the other side of the circle.

The Hadaoui's assistant wandered about, stooping now and then to collect the money, which he placed in a leather pouch. He wore sandals and jeans that had once been white and a thin Moroccan shirt with tiny cotton buttons that ran halfway down the front. He had wavy black hair and was taller than Akari the Estate Agent and the other Moroccan men I knew. As the people dispersed, Khadija jumped up and ran on to the carpet where the old man still sat, quietly smoking. She took a red plastic flower from its pot and presented it to the man who was collecting coins. He looked at her for a moment. I held my breath. Then he smiled and bent down to accept it. Khadija ran about under my jealous stare, collecting flowers one by one and standing straight and still to present them, while the assistant, sharing her solemnity, accepted them with a ritual nod of his head. I hovered in my place, envying her bare feet as they padded over the carpet, until, unable to resist a moment longer, I slipped off my plastic sandals and skidded across to join her. The man smiled quizzically as I handed him my first flower. He looked over my head and I saw his eye meet my mother's and so identify me as her child and a foreigner despite my caftan and dusty feet.

Khadija and I watched as the doves were collected one by one and replaced in their cardboard box. 'We've got a pet,' I said to her. 'Not a dove. A hen.' I pointed at the cooing boxes. 'At home. Would you like to see?'

Khadija shook her head, but I could tell she didn't understand. 'Mum, Mum,' I shouted as I ran towards her. 'What's Arabic for hen?' But I stopped before I got there because she was deep in conversation with the magic

27

man's assistant. They were talking in a mixture of French and English and laughing. They turned to me as I ran up.

'There you are,' she said. 'I saw you earlier on, helping Bilal.'

Bilal smiled at me. He had the most beautiful smile of all smiles and his dark eyes twinkled in a face smooth and without a trace of anything unfriendly. It was then that I noticed the necklace. It hung around his neck in a string of silver and gold beads.

'Mum,' I said, willing her to bend down so I could whisper in her ear, and when she finally did I pressed my face close to hers and said, 'Is Bilal my Dad?'

She stood up and took my hand and patted it.

'Goodbye,' she said, a little abruptly, 'maybe we'll see you here tomorrow.'

'Oh yes,' Bilal answered. 'Tomorrow. Inshallah. God willing.' And he began to roll up the carpet.

The Hadaoui, Bilal and the white doves stayed in Marrakech for a week, attracting a large crowd every afternoon. Each day Khadija and I waited impatiently for the entertainment to end so we could take up our important role as official helpers to Bilal. The old man remained forever too full of mystery and magic to approach. I kept to the edges of the carpet and avoided meeting his eye.

'When you're old, will you turn into the Hadaoui?' I asked Bilal on the afternoon of his last performance.

'I am the Hadaoui. Now. You don't believe me?' he said in his funny broken English.

'But you're not magic,' Bea said.

'And you don't have a beard.'

Bilal laughed. 'Maybe children can tell about these things. Today the Hadaoui stops here. And from tomorrow I am working as a builder.'

'Here? Staying here?'

'Yes. The Hadaoui must have a holiday. So I become a builder. Here in Marrakech.'

I looked over at Mum to see if she was as excited as me that Bilal wasn't to be going away. She was smiling, but she looked as if she might have known all along.

Bilal came to live with us in the Mellah. Every morning he went out early to work on a building site. In the afternoons when it was too hot to work he took us to the square. Best of all he liked to watch the acrobats. There were a troupe of boys, all about seven or eight years old, dressed in red and green silk like little dragons, who did double somersaults from a standing position and tricks so daring the people gasped and clapped and threw coins into a hat. Bilal instructed us to watch them very carefully.

One day over lunch in our cool tiled kitchen Bilal revealed his plan. 'We will have our own show in the Djemaa El Fna!' he declared triumphantly. Bilal was to be Ring Master. Mum was to make the costumes from silk on the sewing-machine we'd brought with us from England, and Bea and I would be the star guests, performing acrobatic tricks. 'People will love to see the English children do the tricks.' Bilal's eyes sparkled. 'We will have a crowd as big as the Hadaoui and we will collect many coins.'

'But I can't do any tricks,' I said, frightened of diminishing his enthusiasm, but unable to restrain my anxiety.

'Bea can you do any tricks? At all?'

Bea shook her head. 'I can do a handstand.'

Bilal was undeterred. 'I train you. We start today. Very soon you will be doing this.' He demonstrated with a backward somersault right there in the kitchen.

That afternoon we dressed in shorts and T-shirts and spread a blanket over the paving-stones. 'Soon,' Bilal said, 'you won't be needing any carpet.'

We started with roly-polies. Head over heels. The names

29

made Bilal laugh. Our attempts to perfect this simple trick did not. My version of a roly-poly was a slow tumble which culminated in a star, as I lay flat on my back, my legs and arms stretched in different directions, staring up at the sky. The best part of it, I thought.

'You must end up on your feet.' Bilal frowned. 'Watch me.' From a standing position Bilal took a couple of quick steps, then, tucking in his head, rolled through the air, his bent back barely touching the ground, and he was upright again. 'You see,' he said. 'A flying rolly-polly.'

We kept working at it. Bilal was patient and encouraging. As part of our training he took us regularly to the square, where we sat and watched the acrobats. For me they had taken on a new majesty. They were tiny and fluid and without fear. They cartwheeled through hoops, formed themselves into pyramids and triple-somersaulted off the top, their bodies bending in half as they flew through the air. I imagined Bea and myself dressed in silk, our hair plaited out of the way, dextrous and skilful, taking a bow to the applauding crowd. We would have so many coins to collect that when we sent enough to Bilal's family in the mountains so that he didn't have to work on the building site any more, there would still be some left over. I took hold of Bilal's hand. 'I promise to practise every day, because ...' And I felt a rush of excitement as the beginnings of a great plan unravelled in my mind. 'Because I've decided that when I grow up I want to be a tightrope walker. You won't tell anyone, will you?'

Bilal nodded. Bilal was someone I could trust.

That afternoon we walked home through the busy streets. I sat on Bilal's shoulders high up above the crowd and from time to time I asked him to let go of my legs so that I could practise balance.

We began going to the park for our training. Mum thought it would be better to practise acrobatic tricks on grass. As the weeks went by, our bodies didn't turn into the fearless, weightless ones Bilal had hoped they would. Or at least Bea's did a little more than mine, but not enough. We began to spend more and more time playing leapfrog, which anyone could do, or lying on the grass telling stories.

Bilal continued to work on the building site. I realized that in order to be a tightrope walker I didn't necessarily have to be an acrobat. So I kept to my own secret plan and practised balancing whenever I got the chance.

CHAPTER SIX

As promised, Bilal took us to visit his family in the mountains. We travelled through a whole day on a bus packed with people and then shared a taxi with a man Bilal knew and was happy to see. We had presents of a large packet of meat and three cones of white sugar for Bilal's mother.

The whole village was waiting to greet us at the end of a narrow track that joined the road. 'They welcome you like a wife,' Bilal whispered as Mum stepped out of the taxi. She was dressed in a swirling blue cloak of material that covered her hair and swathed her body in folds that reached the floor. When she walked she drew up the cloth and let it hang over her shoulder.

Bilal introduced us to his mother. She was a large lady with a throaty voice that billowed out from under her veil. Bilal's father was really an old man and half her size.

The women threw flower petals into the air and sang a low lilting song as we walked back along the path. From time to time they let their fingers brush against my hair. I held tightly on to my mother's hand.

The village was a cluster of low white houses at the foot of a hill that was almost a mountain. We followed Bilal into the dark inside of his family's house. Bilal's family trooped in after us, and we all stood about smiling. Bea nudged Mum and she remembered and handed over the meat and the sugar.

'You see, she likes the presents,' Bilal whispered as his mother nodded, unwrapping and rewrapping her gifts. I had tried to convince him that she might prefer a Tintin book or a clay drum.

That night Mum, Bilal, Bea and I all slept on rugs in the room that was the house, and Bilal's parents, his brothers and sisters, their wives and children all slept outside in the garden. It was a clear warm night and very light from so many stars.

'I wish we could sleep in the garden too,' I said to Bea and she agreed.

'Where's Abdul?' Bea asked next morning over breakfast. We were drinking coffee sweetened with the sugar we had brought. Abdul was Bilal's youngest brother and the same age as Bea. We had tried to teach him hopscotch the evening before.

'Abdul goes to look after the sheep,' Bilal said. 'He is up before the sun.'

'Where?' I asked, looking round for even a single sheep.

'On the other side of the mountain.' Bilal pointed into the hazy distance. 'Over there are all the sheep of the village.'

'Are there other people helping?'

'No, just Abdul.'

So Abdul was a shepherd. I had seen a shepherd that wasn't old and frozen and on the front of a Christmas card. By lunchtime he was back from his day's work. He sat with the sun on his back and ate bread and tajine, his feet covered in dust from the long walk home.

'Bea, would you like to be a shepherd?' I asked her.

'No, not really.'

'What would you like to be then?'

'I don't know. Normal, I think.' She was marking out a new game of hopscotch with the toe of her plastic sandal.

*

33

The next morning when I woke, Bea was not there. Mum was sitting on the end of my bed sewing.

'She went into the hills.'

'When?'

'At sunrise. She wanted to see what it was like to be a shepherd.'

I was close to tears. 'But you knew I wanted to go.'

'I did try and wake you.'

I wasn't sure whether or not to believe her. 'Wouldn't I wake up?'

'No,' she said. 'You just started talking in your sleep.'

'Did I?' I cheered a little at this. I liked the idea of talking in my sleep. 'What did I say? Please remember.'

'Something about roofracks, I think,' she said, folding up the dress she was making for Akari the Estate Agent's little girl. He said it could be rent until our money arrived from England. Roofrack. That was a good word. Roofrack. Roofrack. Hideous kinky. Maybe we could teach Abdul to play tag.

It was midday and I sat at the edge of the village and waited for them to come down from the hills. Eventually two specks turned into stripes and then into Bea and Abdul, both barefoot and in shorts. I ran to meet them. As I neared, I stuck out my hand and, touching Bea's shoulder, shouted, 'Roofrack!' Picking up speed, I circled away for the inevitable chase. I ran hard for a few minutes before I realized she wasn't following. I looped back round, keeping a little distance in case it was a trick.

'Aren't you playing?'

'Of course not,' she said. 'I've been working, haven't I?' And she marched on towards the village.

I followed them to where lunch was being served. The whole family ate from one enormous bowl. It was couscous with a sauce of seven vegetables. I tried to copy the exact movement of Bilal's hand as he collected the tiny grains of couscous in the crook of his finger, swept them into a

34

ball with his thumb, and placed it in his mouth without a crumb being spilt or wasted.

'Tomorrow can I go to the mountains with Abdul?' I asked him when the meal was over.

Bilal shook his head. 'No. Because tomorrow we are going to the festival of the marabouts.'

The festival was a little like a market.

'What's a marabout?' I wanted to know.

Mum pointed out a small white building with a domed roof and a bolt on the door. 'Marabouts are holy men, like saints, who live in these little houses.'

'Is he in there now?'

Mum wasn't sure. She asked Bilal.

'Oh yes. He's in there.'

'Will he come out once the festival starts?'

Bilal looked amused. 'No. It is only his spirit we celebrate.'

We walked towards the building. I peered on tiptoe over the white wall surrounding it.

'For many years,' Bilal said, 'he is lying dead inside.'

Mum and I both pulled away.

Bilal's brothers were erecting a large white tent. It was a tent like others that were going up around the edges of the festival. Round and cool inside. The women from each section of the family were laying out rugs and cotton spreads of material to sleep on. They sat and talked from under their veils while their smallest children slept.

'They wanted Mum to wear a veil,' Bea whispered.

'Who did?'

'The mother and the brothers and everyone else.'

'Why didn't she then?'

'She said she wouldn't.'

'Are they angry?' I looked over at the women resting, their eyes sharp above a square of black.

'It's hard to tell,' Bea said.

35

If you stood very close to the veil you could see through the black and tell whether someone was wearing lipstick or not. I wondered if it was a special magic cloth.

'Nylon,' Mum said when I asked her.

When I woke, Ahmed had arrived. Ahmed was Bilal's brother-in-law.

'Ahmed is married to Bilal's sister,' Mum explained.

'No,' Bilal corrected her. 'Ahmed is divorced from my sister.'

Ahmed had two other wives with him and several children. They spread out their belongings near to ours and the youngest wife tried to settle her baby who was crying. As she wrestled with her child, her veil floated up and I saw her face. She was pale and looked a little like Bilal's sister Fatima who was fourteen and wearing a veil for the first time.

The baby kept on crying. Ahmed's other wife took it from her and began to walk around the tent, rocking and soothing it with words.

Bea and I wandered out into the warm night. The circle of white tents had grown, stretching away round the marabout's shrine. Outside each tent fires were burning and meat roasted on twisting sticks. Ahmed, Bilal and Mum sat by our fire. They were smoking a clay pipe. Passing it from one to another in a circle.

Ahmed began to sing. His voice was sad. He sang the Egyptian songs that played in the outdoor cafés in Marrakech. His voice rose and fell and caught in his throat with such pure sorrow that I was surprised not to see tears running down his face. Bilal joined in on a lower note with a smile on his lips as if to say it wasn't his sad story he was singing.

I crawled on to Mum's lap and basked in the melancholy music and the warmth of the fire. The sour smell from the burning pipe mingled with the roasting meat

36

turning on its spit. It looked like a sheep and I wondered whether or not it was one of Abdul's. If it was, I decided, thinking of Snowy, I would refuse to eat it. Much later that night, when the singing had spread from tent to tent and supper was finally ready, I forgot about my earlier resolutions and, along with Abdul, held out my hands for a kebab.

Mum washed my feet and hands in a bowl of cold water and insisted I change into my nightie. Abdul and his cousins were sleeping where they'd fallen, wrapped tight in their djellabas.

'Can I have some powder on my feet, please?' I asked, as much to keep Mum in the tent as to feel it, silky smooth between my toes.

She took a tin of Johnson's baby powder out of her bag and sprinkled me a ration. Ahmed's youngest wife, still rocking her tireless baby, watched us darkly from behind her veil. As I patted each toe dry, she laid her baby down and slowly unwrapped its clothes, revealing a damp red ring around its neck. Mum leant over and offered her the tin. She stared uncomprehending, until Mum shook a fine layer of white on to the baby's neck. She smoothed it gently and the crying seemed to quiet a little. The lady held on to Mum's hand. 'Thank you, thank you,' she said in Arabic.

Mum pressed the tin into the woman's hands. 'Sprinkle a little every day,' she said, pointing at the baby.

'What about me?' I hissed at her.

'Shh.'

'But it's our only tin.'

Mum glared.

I put my head under the blanket. 'I want Bilal,' I wailed. When I refused to come out even to kiss her goodnight she relented a little and promised to ask Linda to bring some powder with her when she came to visit.

'When will that be?' I asked.

Mum tucked me in and sneaked a butterfly kiss that tickled before going out to rejoin the party.

'Who's Linda, anyway?' I asked Bea, when she eventually came to bed.

'You know ... Linda.' Bea said.

'Linda?'

But Bea said she'd only tell me if I told her a story first and by the time I'd finished 'The Adventures of a Spooky Carpet' she was asleep.

There was everything for sale at the festival. Donkey-loads of water melons, pomegranates, blood oranges – the insides of which you could suck out through a hole in the skin. There was a stall with hundreds of pairs of babouches, the softest most beautiful shoes. They were mostly in yellow or light brown leather but some were black and patterned with stars of silver or gold. There was one pair, red with a zigzag of green, the toes of which curled up like magicians' slippers, that made my eyes burn with wanting them. I was frightened to pick them up or even touch them, and the old man who sat among his slippers gave me no smile of encouragement.

'If you could have any babouches you wanted in the whole world, which ones would you choose?' I asked Mum.

She bent down to finger the leather. 'I was thinking of making you and Bea some sandals ...' she said.

My heart fell.

'Out of leather. With rubber soles. They'll be very nice.'

'But they won't be like these.'

'No, they won't be quite like these,' she said, and she drew me away.

By that evening news of Mum's miracles with the baby powder had spread throughout the tent.

'Oh yes, she is the wise woman from the West,' Bilal said proudly, and he put his arm around her.

'There is a lady Ahmed wants you to help,' Bilal told Mum on our last night around the fire. Ahmed had been particularly impressed by the baby-powder cure. 'He has invited us to visit with him.'

The white tent came fluttering down. We said goodbye to Bilal's family who we would see again in a few days, and to Fatima who was my favourite sister and Abdul. We set off in a different direction with Ahmed and his two wives and their children. The baby's rash had almost vanished, but it still screamed unceasingly. No one took the slightest bit of notice.

During our journey on a bus crowded with people who had all been at the festival, Ahmed explained through Bilal what he wanted Mum to do. 'There is an aunt of Ahmed,' he said, 'who is sad because she has lost her favourite nephew in a car crash. Since he is dead she will not be happy to live.'

'But what does he want me to do?' Mum asked.

Bilal didn't translate her doubts to Ahmed. 'Just talk with her,' he said, smiling assuredly. 'Just visit and talk with her.'

The old lady lived in a room at the back of Ahmed's house, which was large and airy with tiled floors and slatted shutters covering the windows, filtering in just enough light to see. Ahmed wanted Mum to go to her right away.

'I want to come too,' I said. I wouldn't let go of her hand. I couldn't let go. She mustn't go alone into a dark room with a woman who wanted to die, I thought. She might never come out again.

'Stay with the women,' Mum ordered.

I looked over at the silent veiled wives who waited for me, and my breath caught in my throat. 'Please,' I appealed, my voice wild. 'Bilal, tell her please.'

Mum stood unsure. I could feel her staring at me. 'It's just that they're tired,' she said, and we all walked in silence round to the back of the house.

The old lady was lying in her bed when Ahmed ushered us into the room. Startled by the light, she sat up. Her face was striped with thin lines of dried black blood where she had dragged her nails hard across it. My mother sat on the edge of the bed and rummaged in her bag. She pulled out a large bound book. It was her copy of the *I Ching*. She undid the twist in the velvet pouch Bilal had made for her and poured the three large coins into her hand, warming them in her palm as she always did before she told a fortune. Ahmed's aunt watched her with a glimmer of light in her yellow eyes. Mum handed her the coins. They were Arabic coins with stars on one side and the head of the King on the other.

'I want you to throw the coins for me,' Mum said. Bilal spoke to the aunt softly in Arabic and she scattered the three coins on to the bedspread with a thin worn hand.

Mum made a line in pencil in the back of the book and nodded for her to throw again. The old lady threw the coins six times and Mum made a pattern of six broken and unbroken lines, three on each side of a space.

Mum opened the book. The old lady was sitting a little straighter with her shawl held tightly around her shoulders. Mum began to read. 'Persistence brings good fortune. It will be of advantage to cross the great river. The Superior Man will pass this time in feasting and enjoyment ...' Bilal translated in a low murmur as she read and the old lady blinked in concentration with her head slightly on one side. Mum read on and on about lakes and rivers and turning-points until my mind began to wander away from the room.

'Do you think we'll get a chapter of *Bluebeard* tonight?' I whispered.

'Shhh.'

'We haven't had any story for ages.'

The reading was over. There was a silence. Then the old lady smiled and, looking towards Ahmed, commanded him in a startlingly strong voice to bring mint tea and bread. Ahmed hurried out like a small boy. I could hear him shouting out the order as he ran through the house.

Once she had drunk a glass of tea and chewed at the soft inside of a roll, the old lady pushed back the covers and began to climb out of bed. Ahmed smiled a tender smile as her narrow feet touched the floor. She walked slowly over to a painted chest which stood under the window and, opening it, took out a sky-blue caftan. She reached up and held it against my mother's shoulders.

'Thank you,' my mother said, taking it from her.

With the faintest of smiles the old lady climbed back into bed and motioned for us all to go away.

It was mid-morning when we arrived back in Bilal's village. I could see Fatima standing in the doorway of her father's house. I waved and began to run towards her, but instead of coming to meet us she turned and darted inside letting the curtain fall across the door.

'Fatima,' Bilal called after her. 'Fatima,' he ordered, and she reappeared, limping slightly and with a split across her lip.

'What happened to you?' Mum gasped, but Bilal took his sister roughly by the shoulders and began to question her in a voice which shook with anger. Fatima spoke a few tearful words with her head bowed and her eyes on the ground.

'What's happened?'

'It's nothing,' Bilal said. 'Let's get inside.'

The familiar cool of the house had turned so cold it made me shiver. Finally Bilal spoke. 'It is important that Fatima will not make bad her reputation. If she is not good, she will not be married.'

Mum was silent. She looked at him with cold, accusing eyes.

'Fatima has behaved very badly at the festival,' he said. 'Yes?'

'She was seen without her veil – watching the dancing. At night she must stay inside the tent.'

'So she was beaten,' Mum said flatly.

I looked over at Fatima, huddled in the corner, her fingers moving through a bowl of string beans.

'My brothers tied her in the barn and beat her . . .' Bilal looked away, ashamed, then added, 'But now she will be good and then she will be married.'

Fatima lifted the bowl in her arms and hobbled silently to the back door.

Mum watched her go. 'I think maybe it's time to go home,' she said.

'Tomorrow,' Bilal insisted. 'Stay until tomorrow and we will all go back to the Mellah.'

CHAPTER SEVEN

Bilal could not find any work in Marrakech. The Hadaoui
was still on holiday and our money had not arrived at the
bank. 'I have friends in Casablanca who have work,' he
said, 'they are expecting me.'

'Casablanca. Where's that? Can I come?'

'I'll come back and visit.' Bilal knelt down so I could
climb on to his back. I clung to him as he wandered
around the house gathering up his things.

Bilal left with one half-empty bag, dressed in the same
faded clothes I'd first seen him in. We stood by the garden
wall and waved to him until he disappeared.

That night we ate supper in the kitchen. We didn't go
out to the square as we usually did. No one even mentioned
going.

'If our money doesn't come this week,' Mum said, 'we'll
have to move.'

'What'll happen to Snowy if we move?' Bea's voice was
a challenge.

'We'll take her with us,' Mum soothed, but absent-
mindedly. She lit the paraffin lamp with a twist of paper.

'Couldn't you make Akari's little girl another dress?' I
asked.

Mum didn't think so.

'Luigi Mancini,' Bea said in a flash of inspiration. 'Let's
go and visit Luigi Mancini.'

'Maybe he'll give us lots of money!' I shrieked.

Bea kicked me under the table.

Mum was thinking. 'Yes we could visit Luigi Mancini.' She ran the idea over in her head. 'But don't you dare ask him for any money. Do you understand?'

We all agreed that this was the exact spot where Luigi Mancini's palace had stood. Now there was nothing here but a thin, dry wood of larches that rustled eerily in the late afternoon. We walked back to the taxi. It was a horse-drawn taxi with two horses.

'Luigi Mancini . . .?' Bea tried for the hundredth time to ignite a flicker of recognition in our driver, but he shook his head sadly.

'We passed through this village and took a turning to the right,' Mum insisted, even though we'd tried every turning, right and left, within miles of the village. This village that had mysteriously never heard the name Luigi Mancini. By the time we gave up the search it was almost night.

'A genie must have cast a spell,' I said, 'that picked up his house and garden and all the peacocks and moved them to a different place. He probably woke up one morning and looked out of his window to find he was in Casablanca or on the top of a mountain or in England, a bit like – '

'The Wizard of Oz,' Bea interrupted in her most bored voice.

'Will you shut up both of you,' Mum snapped and she leant back in the taxi and closed her eyes.

A week later we moved into the Hotel Moulay Idriss. It stood in a narrow street behind the Djemaa El Fna and was built around a courtyard of multipatterned tiles in the centre of which grew a banana tree that was taller than the top floor. Snowy would have loved to play among

44

the tree roots and make dust baths in the earth, but the only room they had to offer was on the second floor. It was a large room with two doors that looked out on to the courtyard and no window. We brought our mattresses from the Mellah to sit and sleep on and Mum set up a kitchen in one corner with the mijmar. The leaves from the banana tree cast a soft green shadow.

Bea made a nest for Snowy with straw. She encouraged her to sit in it and maybe even lay an egg, but Snowy wanted to explore. She set off at a run along the landing that linked the rooms on all four sides of the hotel.

'All right, I'll train her to find her own way home.' And Bea scattered liberal handfuls of corn over both our doorsteps. Snowy liked the Hotel Moulay Idriss. Soon she was striding about with confidence, clucking and pecking her way into other people's rooms and leaving little piles of yellow-white droppings wherever she went.

Next door lived a family with five children, and a grandmother who slooshed down her stretch of landing first thing each morning with water from a metal bucket. Each time Snowy dared to pass her by, she hissed and shooed and flicked the ground with the edge of her djellaba.

Once the corridor was dry, a girl, not much taller than Bea, appeared. She stood patiently on the landing to be checked over by the fierce old lady. Her hair was braided into two plaits and she wore a white pleated skirt and sandals. Over one shoulder she carried a leather satchel.

'Where's she going?' Bea asked.

'Who?' Mum said sleepily.

'The girl next door. Come and look.'

'I expect she's just going to school.' Mum stretched out under the covers and then in a coaxing voice she said, 'If you make some strong tea with sugar in, I'll get up. I promise.'

*

45

The next morning we were woken by the lady who lived in the room on our other side. She stood in the doorway and shouted, loud enough to wake the whole hotel. She held a dark red sequinned cushion in one hand, carefully like a tray, on which was a murky yellow stain. She pointed an accusing finger at Snowy who sat innocently in her nest of straw, chattering happily, her feathers up around her neck. The woman stood there, holding out her cushion and shouting. Mum struggled out of bed and tried to reason with her, but the woman continued to point at the cushion, at Bea, and at herself, and then with a vicious kick in Snowy's direction she swept out of the room. Bea rushed over and picked Snowy up in her arms. Her eyes were spinning with alarm. The woman's shouts of fury continued through the dividing wall.

Mum sat on the end of Bea's bed. 'It looks like we're going to have to find Snowy another home.'

Bea didn't answer. Then she said in a very small voice, 'I'll train her.'

'I'll talk to Akari,' Mum said. 'He'll know what to do.'

That afternoon Akari came and took Snowy away.

'I will look after her. Very special,' he beamed as he hurried down the corner stairs.

We refused to return his smile. 'Like hell,' Bea said under her breath.

The only people who commiserated with us on the loss of our pet were the two women who lived on the opposite side of the landing. When they saw Akari disappear down the stairs with Snowy clucking her last in a cardboard box, they came across and offered Mum Turkish cigarettes and a glass of wine. They were big women who wore brightly coloured djellabas with silky hoods halfway down their backs, and their hands and feet were covered in an intricate web of design.

'Tattoos,' Bea whispered.

'Henna,' the woman nearest me laughed, noticing my fascinated stare. She took my face and held it still with one hand, while with the fingers of the other she twisted a strand of my hair between her fingers. It made a dry, brittle sound in her hand like the scratching of an insect. 'Henna,' she said, turning to Mum and switching to French to convince her.

'They say you need henna on your hair to make it grow thick and long.'

I looked at their heavy black plaits.

'All right,' I agreed.

I was taken through the curtain into the dark recess of their room. It smelt of perfume and night-time, as if they had lived in it for ever. Bea was sent to get a towel and to fill a bucket from the tap in the corner of the courtyard. My hair was brushed back off my face in preparation.

The women poured a heap of green powder into a bowl and, with Bea's water, stirred it into a thick mud that smelt like mud but with something sweet and something sour mixed in. They patted the henna, cold and slimy, into every strand of my hair, coiling it up on top of my head so that when they'd finished I felt like I was wearing a soft clay helmet. They dipped the corner of the towel in water and wiped away the streaks of green from my face and ears.

I was led triumphantly back on to the balcony, where Mum was still sipping wine in the sun. She laughed when she saw me.

'Isn't Bea going to have her hair hennaed too?' I asked, desperate suddenly not to be the only one, the only experiment. The women smiled, and as sharply as if I had ordered it they took her inside.

Soon Bea and I were both sitting in the sun, weighed down and sleepy with the mud cakes drying on our heads. We had resigned ourselves to a long, hot day on the terrace of the Hotel Moulay Idriss, watching the comings and goings of the various inhabitants and from time to time catching a glimpse of Moulay Idriss himself when he emerged from the gloom of his office on the ground floor.

'Can I take it off now?' I asked Mum, once she had started to prepare the evening meal, but she shook her head and said, 'It would be best to keep it on until tomorrow morning.'

I began to protest.

'That's what the Ladies said. If you keep it on until the morning, your hair will grow thicker and longer than anyone else's.'

'The morning!'

I sat against the wall between the doors of our room, playing with Mum's box of buttons and beads, thoughts of Rapunzel dancing through my mind, and wondered how I'd be able to get to sleep that night.

The next morning when I tapped at the top of my head it echoed like a clay drum. Mum sent us round to the Ladies to have the henna taken off. The hardest pieces were cracked away, catching and pulling at strands of baked hair, and the rest was soaked out in a bowl of water. The water, when I looked at it, was a dark, steamy red that grew thinner and paler with every rinse. When the water was clear and my hair had been combed straight down on either side of my face, I was sent outside to look at myself in a tiny round mirror.

At first I thought it must only be a reflection of the sun beating down through the banana leaves, but once I'd pulled my hair around in front of my eyes, I was not so sure. I looked at it hard, then again in the mirror, then attempted to match up the two colours, which were in fact one colour. The colour of my hair. Orange.

Still clutching the mirror, I ran along the landing to find Mum.

'Look. They've tricked me,' I sobbed, throwing myself down on the floor. 'It's horrible. I hate it. And I hate them.' And I hate you, I added to myself, for conspiring in this master trick against me.

Mum knelt down and lifted up my face. She pushed the still-damp hair out of my eyes. 'It's beautiful,' she soothed. 'Beautiful. It's a rich dark red, it's copper, it's auburn ...'

'It's orange,' I wept.

'Haven't you noticed,' she continued, 'all the most beautiful girls in Marrakech have hennaed hair?'

I shook my head.

'You haven't noticed? I'll take you for a walk and show you.'

Just then Bea appeared in the doorway. She was a dark shadow in a blazing halo of red and gold.

'What do you think?' she said.

The sun behind her picked out a thousand colours in her hair and set them flying against one another like the fighting flames of a torch.

'It's beautiful,' Mum and I both said in one breath and she squeezed me tight in spite of myself.

CHAPTER EIGHT

'Will you run and bring our towel back,' Mum asked Bea, as we were about to leave for the square. 'And take the Ladies' mirror ... and say thank you,' she shouted after her.

We waited in the courtyard. I had tucked all my hateful hair up inside a hat in the shape of a fez. It was a hat made from cotton covered in tiny holes for cross-stitch, which Bilal had embroidered pink and green before he left for Casablanca. I was hot and I felt Mum's scornful eye on me.

'Come on,' she grumbled.

Finally Bea appeared. 'They won't give it back,' she said.

'What do you mean?'

'The towel. It was hanging in their room but when I tried to take it, they said it belonged to them.'

Mum laughed and looked up at their landing. The curtain hung heavily across the entrance to their room, and even though we waited neither one nor the other appeared.

The square was very busy. We sat outside a café while Mum drank black coffee and Bea and I sucked warm Fanta through a straw. It was unbearably hot under my hat. Little streams of sweat fell down around my ears and into my eyes, but it had been too big a fight to get the hat on to enable me to take it off. I sweated and suffered.

There was a man selling majoun on the corner. He was not always there. Mum bought a piece like a little chunk of rock. She let us both break off a sliver with our teeth. It tasted delicious, like crystallized sugar with soft honeycomb that hid something sharp that made you want more to cover the trace of bitterness.

'Please can we have a piece? Please?' we begged, forced on by the delicious sweetness of it.

'It's not meant for children. It'll make you ...' – she was searching for the word – 'drunk.'

'Please, please,' we insisted. 'Majoun, majoun, majoun,' and we set up a chant rising in volume with every refrain.

'Shhh,' Mum tried to quiet us, frantic, but giggling herself. 'All right you can share a piece, but for God's sake be quiet about it.'

We handed over our dirham and pointed and whispered, 'Majoun,' as we had seen it done. We were handed a twist of newspaper inside which was a small lump of hashish pounded into a sweet like fudge. We sat at the table and took turns scraping fragments off with our teeth. It seemed to me the most delicious taste in the world. Sand mixed with honey and fried in a vat of doughnuts. We passed it back and forth, giggling a conspiracy of joy and adventure.

'Let's make it last for ever,' I said, barely touching it with the tip of my tongue.

'Let's go and see if Luigi Mancini's in town.' Bea slid off her chair.

I glanced at Mum. 'We'll meet back here,' she said.

Looking for Luigi Mancini had become our favourite game. We investigated one café at a time, reporting to each other the movements of any tall man dressed in white. Sometimes we would settle on a particularly suspicious Luigi Mancini look-alike and follow him through his afternoon's business.

'Don't forget,' Bea would say, 'he might have dyed his hair, shaved off his moustache, or given up smoking.'

Today, light-headed and bursting with laughter, it was hard to remain unnoticed by anyone. We crept up staircases, across terraces and around the tables of the largest cafés, whispering 'Luigi Mancini' almost inaudibly, and then standing like statues to monitor the reaction.

Today there was no one who could possibly be mistaken for Luigi Mancini, or even Luigi Mancini's brother. There was no one in the café who was not Moroccan.

Then I heard a woman's voice. 'Excuse me, hello, can anyone speak English? Hello?'

'Listen.' I pulled at Bea's sleeve.

Then we both heard it.

'Hello, do you speak ENGLISH? I'm trying to find ... oh dear ...'

'It's Linda,' Bea said.

'Linda?' But she had already darted off in the direction of the small crowd of waiters that had gathered.

Linda stood surrounded by suitcases, a fat and sleeping baby propped on one hip. She was holding out a crumpled scrap of paper.

'Hello, Linda. What are you doing here?' We squeezed into view between the legs of the onlookers.

Linda sat down on a bulging duffle bag and burst into tears.

'I'll go and get Mum,' Bea said and disappeared.

'What's your baby called?' I asked as she wiped her eyes with toilet paper from a roll.

'Mob,' she said.

'Can I hold it?'

'Her.' She passed the baby over.

As soon as Mob was on my lap she woke up and began to scream.

'Have I met you before?' I asked.

Linda nodded.

'Did you have a baby when I last saw you?' I had to shout over Mob's yells.

'No.'

'How old is she?'

'Six months.'

'Why's she called Mob?'

Linda sighed. 'Because her father was an Anarchist.'

'What's an Anarchist?'

Mum and Bea had arrived. Linda stood up and blew her nose. 'Didn't you get my letter?'

And Mum said, 'Didn't you get mine?'

Then they both began to laugh and hugged each other and we all helped to carry Linda's luggage back to the Hotel Moulay Idriss.

'I bought you a dress with the money you sent.' Linda riffled through her suitcase. 'From Biba.'

We watched as Mum tried it on. It was a soft cotton dress in golden browns and oranges, like a park trampled with autumn leaves. It had bell-shaped sleeves that buttoned at the wrist.

'I love it,' Mum said, spinning around in a dance.

I heaved a private sigh of relief. Surely this meant now she would stop wearing her Muslim haik that turned her into someone's secret wife, with or without a veil.

'You look beautiful.' Linda was still heaping clothes on to the floor.

'Yes, beautiful, beautiful,' I agreed, eager to encourage.

Bea didn't say anything. Her face was set and worried.

'And I bought these for you.' Linda held out a pair of faded black trousers. 'From the Portobello Road.'

I gasped with excitement as I tried them on. They even had a zip.

'Do I look like a boy?'

'Not really.' Mum was rolling up the legs in thick wedges round my ankles.

53

'I thought she'd have grown ...' Linda said.

'Not even with my hat?' I looked around for it. In my excitement I had forgotten the horror of my orange hair.

Bea had a striped T-shirt that was long enough to be a dress. It had a hole under one arm.

'Are you Linda who was going to bring the baby powder?' I asked.

Bea jumped up. 'So you did know she was coming. You did know.' She turned on Mum.

'I didn't know exactly when ...'

Bea's face was dark. 'You should have told me.'

'I'm sorry.' Linda looked as if she were going to cry again.

'Don't be silly.' Mum held Bea at arm's length. 'Everything will be fine. Linda and Mob can stay here. There's plenty of room.'

'There's plenty of room.' Bea mimicked, almost under her breath but loud enough to strangle the air in the room. Mob gurgled in Linda's arms and was sick. Linda mopped it up with toilet roll.

'In the toilets in Morocco they only have a water tap and sometimes they just have stones,' I told her.

Bea walked out on to the landing and hung her head over the railings. It was beginning to grow dark and the grey shadows outside, for a moment, exactly matched the half-light in the room. Mum lit a lamp and Bea disappeared into sudden darkness.

She kicked at the door-frame as she came back in. 'I have to start school,' she said.

Relief clouded my mother's face. 'Of course. Well you can.'

'How can I?' Bea was unimpressed. 'I need a white skirt – which I don't have. I need a white shirt – which I don't have. I need a satchel.' She stood in the middle of the room, victorious. 'You see. I can't.'

'Tomorrow first thing we'll go to the bank and see if

our money has arrived and if it has we'll buy you a uniform before we do anything else.'

'And if it hasn't?'

'We'll just have to wait a few days.'

'And if it still hasn't?'

'We'll think of something,' Mum promised.

'Will you think of something for me as well?' I asked.

'You don't want to go to school.' Her voice was decisive where it concerned me. 'School is for big girls like Bea and Ayesha next door.'

CHAPTER NINE

A few days turned into a few more days and Mum borrowed some money from Linda. We went to the market to choose material. A large piece of white cotton. We left Bea to bargain for it while we waited at the next stall.

'How did she learn to speak Arabic like that?' Linda asked, as Bea haggled over the price.

Mum and I exchanged vague looks. 'She just seemed to pick it up.'

'Bea does all the shopping now,' I told her, 'because she's got brown eyes and mine and Mum's are green.'

'They think she's a little Moroccan girl,' Mum explained. 'We save a lot of money that way.'

Mum sat at home all that day and into the night sewing a pleated skirt and a white shirt with short sleeves. Ayesha was invited into our room so that Mum could inspect her uniform. She brought her schoolbook with her.

'It must be my turn to look at it now,' I whined when it seemed to have gone round the room at least twice. Ayesha watched anxiously as we pored over her book. On the front were two children: a boy and a girl. They were holding hands and about to take a step. The girl had a bright yellow dress against a red background and the boy was red on yellow. They both had short black hair. On the first page there were pictures of animals in different coloured squares.

'Wasp, bat, ant, crocodile.' I held my breath for a scorpion.

'You're meant to say them in Arabic, stupid.' Bea started to rattle through the animals. She had a little help from Ayesha. Tortoise, for example. There were pages and pages of animals and objects of every kind. Telephones, syringes, shoes. All in coloured boxes and some of them had black squiggles above.

'What's this?' I pointed to the black.

'That's Arabic writing. That,' Mum pointed, 'presumably means snail.'

'Are you going to learn to read in Arabic?' I asked Bea in amazement.

'Yes,' she said. 'I already know that you have to start from the right of the page.'

I bowed my head. I wished I knew what side that was.

'Look, there's a picture of a girl with blonde hair.' I leafed through for an orange one. 'Why are all the people dressed in English clothes?' There was one picture of a boy in a djellaba and a round cap but he was a shepherd and he wasn't at school. He was on a mountain like Abdul, surrounded by sheep.

As soon as Bea's clothes were ready she started school. My heart was swollen with envy and pride and fear for her. Mum, Linda, Mob and I watched her set off, hand in hand with Ayesha, her stiff white clothes standing out around her like wrapping. Even Ayesha's grandmother gave us a smile as she shook her rugs into the courtyard.

'My nappies,' Linda suddenly shrieked. 'My nappies have gone. I hung them out last night. Five nappies and a vest.'

'Here's the vest,' I said. It was still hanging on the railing. 'It's dry.'

'Maybe they fell into the courtyard,' Mum suggested.

Linda was already heading for the stairs.

57

'They're not here,' she bawled up a minute later, drawing several people out on to the landing. 'Has anyone seen NAPPIES?' Linda shouted to them. 'NAPPIES?' She drew a square in the air with her hands.

I crouched in the doorway. Icy with embarrassment. The Henna Ladies had come out and were watching from their landing. They waved at me.

I heaved Mob up in my arms and took her inside as my excuse.

'You don't mind, do you?' I looked down into her pale blue eyes. 'About nappy thieves?'

Mob and I sat side by side on the mattress that was now my and Bea's bed and listened to the high-pitched shrieks and bitter explanations as Linda interrogated one after another of the inhabitants of the hotel.

'When we go out can I carry Mob on my back like the girls in the square?'

Linda was still distracted over her loss.

'You know Khadija? And the beggar girls in the Djemaa El Fna?'

'Yes,' Linda said.

'Well, they carry their baby brothers and sisters around on their backs. They tie them on with a piece of material. We could use a bedspread.'

Linda was counting through her pile of remaining nappies in varying shades of grey and white. 'All right, if you really want to,' she agreed.

A bell was being rung as we waited at the gates of Bea's school. Children began to appear.

I pulled out the bedspread. 'Will you tie her on now?'

I stood with my feet squarely apart to keep from being toppled over by the wriggling weight. Mob's damp towelling body pressed against my back as she was knotted tightly on, over one shoulder and across my chest. I sweated to think of Khadija gliding through the crowds, her bundle of baby borne lightly as a shawl. I longed to sit down.

At that perfect moment Bea appeared. I took a few unsteady steps towards her. Mob began to yell and pull my hair.

'Bea! Yoo-hoo!' Mum and Linda waved and called to attract her attention.

My legs were beginning to shiver with the strain. Bea took one look at me and I heard like a prayer, 'Can I have a go?'

I twisted up my mouth and paused for as long as I could bear. 'Seeing as it's your first day ...' I said, and I sat down heavily and too fast and began fumbling with the knot.

Mob was transferred to Bea's back and we set off for lunch in the square. I watched her face for signs of strain, and was soon rewarded by a definite loss of colour, a breathy voice, dawdling behind, and 'She's quite heavy, isn't she?'

There was a burst of laughter. 'Well, you lasted five minutes longer than your sister.' Linda tweaked her cheek. 'She's not been fed on Heinz baby food for nothing.'

As we dipped bread into the circles of olive oil that floated on our scalding bowls of soup, Bea told about her day.

'We sat in a room and copied everything the teacher said. One girl got beaten with a stick.'

Mum was horrified. 'Why?'

'Because she peed in the classroom. The teacher beat her until the stick broke, and then when the stick broke everyone was very happy, and then a boy from the school next door who is her favourite boy brought over a new stick.'

'My God.' Mum put her head in her hands.

'Are you going to go again tomorrow?' I asked.

59

'Of course.' Bea was adamant.

'Linda had five nappies stolen.' I wanted her to know what she'd missed. 'Mum thinks it might be the Henna Ladies.'

'No, I do not. They probably just blew away.'

Linda muttered under her breath and fed Mob another piece of bread. 'Prostitutes,' she hissed.

CHAPTER TEN

Each morning I dressed in my black trousers and tucked my hair up into a hat. I was keeping watch for Bilal. I waited in the courtyard, amusing myself by walking along the white lines between the tiles, precariously balancing, one foot in front of the other, as if it were a tightrope. I was also on the lookout for stray nappies. Every day, whatever time of day or night Linda hung out her washing, when she came to take it in, at least one nappy would be missing. I was sure I had seen one of the Henna Ladies coming out of the downstairs toilet wearing one on her head like a turban. So far not one had been recovered.

'If things carry on like this I shall have to think of going home,' Linda said more than once.

I woke to the pounding on wood of feet and fists, and the screaming voice of a woman. I jumped up. Linda was not in her bed. Mum sat up sleepily, but on hearing the roar that was beginning to build outside, she sprang up and rushed out in her nightie. I watched her race round to where Linda was hammering. She was beating on the closed door of the Henna Ladies — the Nappy Thieves. She was shouting for them to come out. Ayesha's grandmother hobbled out on to the landing. She stumbled to help drag Linda away. Linda clung, swearing, to the railings, and then the door opened and the two women stepped out, draped in bright silk, their hair loose.

'Quick, Bea, come and look,' I screamed.

The gallery was a flurry of cloth and hair and the woman from our left whose cushion had been ruined was hurling slippers at my mother's head. Slippers, fruit, anything she could find. Her husband stood in the doorway and shouted. I looked over the railings for Moulay Idriss to come out of his little room but he was not at home. Mum picked up an orange that rolled along the landing. She held it in her strong hand and flung it back, hitting the cushion woman on the ear with a smack so ferocious that for a moment everything else was quiet.

I dragged on my trousers and ran round along the other side of the landing. I wanted to pull at the skirt of my mother's nightdress and force her back into our room. I wanted her to be still and calm and never go out again. As I ran I slipped and fell, scraping my knee across the stone floor. I curled up on the ground and stared into the jagged cut across my trouser leg. Inside a graze was filling up with blood. I sobbed. Now Bilal would never see my trousers with a zip. I pulled myself up, blind with pity, my forehead swelling to a bruise. I headed for home, forgetting.

There was Mum, dragging the stove from John's broken-down van. She was dragging it through the door. Dragging it with her along the landing. The people shrank away. She was trying to lift it. Throw it. Finally she hurled it. Her hands bleeding. It bounced and scraped along the landing, forcing people back into doorways. She followed in its wake. The blood from her fingers running down her arms. 'Stop it! Stop it!' I could hear myself screaming as if it were someone else's voice. Bea was behind me shouting in Arabic. The metal of the stove still clanked and smashed against the railings.

A hand on my shoulder made me turn and a woman's

arm drew me through a doorway into a lamplit room. Bea and I crouched behind a mound of cushions under a wall thick with hangings. The room was heavy with the clamour of outside and the woman stood in the middle of the room, anxiously watching the door. She was young and beautiful, dressed in a caftan threaded with gold. I had seen her husband, a rich man, waiting his turn to use the toilet by the stairs.

'They want to find out how the poor people live,' Ayesha had told us. 'They have a big house with servants. But now they live here.'

The woman looked at us with gentle eyes. She knelt down and touched the fraying edges of my trousers.

'Take them off,' Bea nudged, in response to the woman's murmurings.

My ears were full of the pounding of the fight behind the door. The echo of it rose and fell in waves. She pulled me up and began carefully to peel away my precious trousers, lifting each foot as she slipped them off. I did nothing to help. She sat me on a stool and washed the cut with water and a soft cloth. She smeared it with bright red cream that looked like blood. I smiled at the gore of it.

'Come through,' she said with her eyes. Bea and I followed her into a smaller room. A baby was sleeping on a bed piled high with cushions, on to which we climbed. From this windowless room only the occasional shout drifted in from outside. The lady brought us glasses of milk and coils of bright orange pastry filled with honey, so sweet it stung your mouth. I lay back on the bed and closed my eyes, flickering my lids against a haunting of my mother's bleeding hands.

I was being carried through bright sunlight. I struggled against strong unfamiliar arms.

'Put me down.' I kicked, and a dark face swam into my vision. Smiling at me.

'Bilal.' I clung to him, my arms twisting round his neck. We were on the landing outside our room. A quiet lunchtime breeze murmured through the hotel – the smell of food behind closed doors. My mother was walking just behind, holding Bea by the hand and carrying my trousers in the other.

'Good afternoon,' she said, as if by chance she hadn't seen me for a long time.

Lunch was spread out on a cloth on the floor. Bilal set me down and admired the red gash on my knee. 'It really, really hurts,' I said, knowing he knew it didn't.

Linda was changing Mob.

'Did you get the nappies back?' Bea asked.

'Only one.' She pointed to a tattered rag soaking in a bucket. 'They were using it as a dishcloth.'

'They've been stealing Mob's nappies to wear as turbans,' I told Bilal.

He laughed as if he knew the story. Then I remembered the gash in my trousers. I pulled them on and looked mournfully at the ruined knee. 'Do you think I look like a boy?'

Bilal ruffled my hair. It was growing thicker and longer as predicted, and the orange of it was not so bright as it had been. Bilal heaped his plate with bread and tomato salad. He turned to Bea. 'So you are a schoolgirl now?'

Bea nodded.

'A schoolgirl who would like a holiday? A holiday on the Barage?'

'But I've only just started.'

Mum scowled at her. 'You'd like to go to the seaside for a few days. Surely?'

'I'll fall behind.'

'She might get hit with a stick,' I chimed in, longing to go.

Bea looked hard at her plate.

'I'll think about it,' she said.

CHAPTER ELEVEN

We packed the food we'd bought into a cardboard box. Packets of rice, chick-peas, tomatoes. A round soft cheese in hard paper. Pomegranates, and a mound of tiny oranges. Mum dressed us both. in loose caftans for the long, hot journey to come.

'We'll have breakfast on the bus,' she said hurrying.

Linda had taken a job typing poems for a blind poet she'd met in the Djemaa El Fna. She and Mob were staying at the hotel. We waved goodbye to Ayesha, the beautiful lady in the gold caftan, and the two nappy thieves who smiled and waved as if life were too short to bear grudges.

Bilal carried the box of food, on top of which sat a saucepan, a bowl and a sharp knife. His bag rattled with cups and a tin-opener. Mum carried the tartan duffle bag, borrowed from Linda, and Bea and I had a blanket each. We walked in procession through the streets.

As our bus pulled out of Marrakech, Bilal took a square of green corduroy from his pocket and straightened it carefully on his knee. 'A patch for your trousers,' he said.

'But I didn't bring them with me.'

Bilal winked in the direction of the duffle bag. He took a mesh of silk embroidery thread and borrowed a needle and a tiny pair of scissors from Mum. I leant against Bilal's arm as he sewed, remembering only now and then to look out of the window, at the flat orange countryside that was gradually turning to sand. A flower began to appear on the corduroy in shimmering blue and green thread, a pink leaf curling round the side of it. As the hours slipped by and the sun beat through the metal walls of the bus, a bird grew, perching on the flower's top in profile, its tiny claws clinging and its beak open in song. The talk and laughter of the other passengers faded away as the driver's recorded prayers turned to harsh readings of the Koran that boomed through the bus at top volume.

The bus jolted to a stop. The driver gave a long shout and turned off the engine. We were in a red and green town. The street was one long arched terrace of rust-coloured houses with green shutters over every window and green tiles in a row just below the flat roof. We shuffled sleepily off the bus. We were expected. Men busily fried skewers of meat over roadside fires, and the small round loaves of bread for sale were still warm. There were hard-boiled eggs with a sprinkling of salted cumin that came separately in newspaper twists and deep-fried sweets made with orange-flower water. Bilal ordered us each a bowl of soup in a painted clay bowl. It was ladled up from a vat above a tiny flame.

'What is it?' Mum asked as we stood by the side of the road and dipped wooden spoons into the brimming white stew.

Bilal tasted it and smiled in delight. He went into a rapturous explanation.

'Tripe,' Mum said when he had finished, and refused to elaborate.

After lunch Bea and I sat in the shade of the arched houses and looked through her book. She was teaching me the animals.

'Which one do you think is a tripe?' I asked.

67

She didn't know. 'It might be a relation of the turnip,' she said, and pointed to another animal whose name I had forgotten.

'Helufa!' I shouted in triumph when we arrived at the pig with the curling tail.

The bus driver, who had started up his bus, blasted alternate warning notes on his two horns, and as he rumbled slowly out of town everyone ran, clinging to the doors, to pull themselves back on.

'Was that the Barage?' I asked Mum.

'No,' she said. 'That was just lunch.'

The Barage was not the seaside but an enormous lake. If you stood on the shore in the early morning before it became too dazzlingly hot, you could see the other side, but for most of the day it was easy to forget there was anything out there at all.

The bus set us down on a sandy stretch of land where pine trees grew in clusters. We were the only people to get off. It was late afternoon and the sand was still hot enough to scorch the soles of your feet. We threw our luggage down at the foot of a tree that was one of a circle of five and Mum began to spread out the rugs and blankets. She made a soft bog of bedding wide enough for us all to sleep in.

Bilal picked up the saucepan and whistled. He turned inland and trudged off through the sand. He also had a large plastic bottle with a screw top and a canvas flask that hung from his belt. Bea and I followed him up the soft slope of the beach into a cool ridge of trees. We walked single-file along a path, taking deep breaths of pine-sweetened air and stamping hard from time to time to watch the salamanders disappear into nowhere. I could see the lake, blue and shimmering a little below me on one side, and on the other the road down which our bus had passed.

Bilal helped us over a low wall into an amber dry field

68

full of sheep. The sheep raised their heads to watch us as we passed. They flicked their lashes against a swarm of flies, and kept their eyes on us. In the corner of the field, shaded by a clump of palm trees, was a high circle of stone.

'A well,' Bea shouted, leaning in. Her voice echoed. 'Well-ell-lll.'

It gave off an ancient damp smell. A shiny black reflection bounced back at me as I stared into its depths. There was a plastic bucket tied to the wall by a length of string. Bilal let the bucket drop. Silence. Then a sharp splash as it hit the water. The bucket floated far away on the surface, sinking slowly until with a tightening of the rope and a sound like a gulp it went under. Bilal pulled it up fast. He set the two bottles and the saucepan on the ground and filled them with great care. I squatted near to watch as not a drop was lost. He offered up his canvas flask for us to drink from. Long, hard swallows of the clear water. It gurgled inside my stomach, pushing it out like a football. Bilal refilled the flask. He tipped the remaining water back into the well.

The camp was deserted. We shouted for Mum, scanning the beach, shading our eyes against the sun which had sunk towards the lake, turning it to gold and spreading shadows from the foot of each tree. I heard laughter and a shout on the breeze. There she was, her arms waving at us from the water.

'She's swimming!' I shouted to Bea.

'Hideous kinky!' she shouted back.

Bilal, Bea and I stood at the edge of the lake, ankle-deep in water, and watched Mum floating on her back.

'Come in,' she said, as if it were her own watery kingdom.

Bilal flung off his clothes and waded out to her. Just before he reached my mother's floating body, he took a dive and swam right under her. She screamed and tipped over. Bilal struck out into the middle of the lake.

'Take everything off,' Mum scolded, as I stepped gingerly into the shallows, one hand clutching at the weak elastic of my knickers. I sat down quickly, the water up to my waist. Mum laughed and flitted about like a mermaid.

I lay in the silky sand letting the waves wash me back and forth. The lake was as warm as a puddle. With one hand I held on to my waterlogged pants and with the other I clutched at any shell or rock large enough to hold me to land each time the waves dragged back into the lake.

'Shall I teach you to swim?' Bea asked.

'No thanks.' I was clinging to a piece of seaweed.

'Doggie paddle.' She splashed up and down in front of me, kicking her legs. 'Watch. Just hold your breath and close your eyes. One two three. Go.'

A few seconds later I opened my eyes. It seemed I had only moved a matter of inches. The water swirled around me thick with sand and tiny shells.

'My pants!' I leapt after them, plunging up to my neck as I grabbed at a dark blue shadow.

'Mum, I've lost my ...' But she had swum out to Bilal and now they were two black specks against the sinking sun.

I fought back to the shallows, the sand slipping from under my feet.

'Mum ...' I shouted over the water. I knew she wouldn't hear me. Tears as warm as the lake trickled down my face.

Bea held up her identical pair of navy pants. I looked at her. She was going to give them to me. Pretend she'd found them. That they were mine. When really they were hers.

But she didn't. She screwed them up into a ball and threw them as far out as she could. We watched them

70

float away on a current.

'Knock, knock,' she said.

'Who's there?'

'Nicholas.'

'Nicholas who?'

'Nicholas girls shouldn't climb trees.'

We screamed with laughter. We lay on our stomachs in the waves and discussed whether we'd prefer to be a water baby or a chimney sweep. And who we'd least like to meet under the sea. Mrs Doasyouwouldbedoneby. Or Mrs Bedonebyasyoudid. I thought I'd prefer to be Tom the chimney sweep once he'd become a water baby. We lay in the lake covered up to the chin. The water was warmer now than the air.

Mum and Bilal rose silently up out of the lake, making us jump.

'Did you swim right the way across?' I asked.

'No, just along the shore a little. Have you seen the sunset?'

I turned around. The sun was a smouldering crescent, lying on the edge of the world. Fingers of light streamed away from it up through a wafer-thin purple cloud and into the dome of the sky. We sat shivering and watched the sun sink, giving up the sky to a moon that had hovered high since late afternoon, waiting for its chance of glory.

CHAPTER TWELVE

'Have you been here before?' I asked Bilal as we sat cross-legged around last night's burnt-out fire, sucking the juice from oranges.

He pointed to the lake. 'You see that?'

I jumped up. A red tractor was gliding noiselessly over the water. It had four enormous wheels that turned mysteriously without sinking. There was someone driving it. A man. And I could see a lady in a pink bikini sitting by his side.

'Is it going to sink?' I had watched it for five minutes, my heart in my mouth.

'It's made from plastic.' Bilal hardly gave it a glance. 'With pedals.'

I shouted for Bea. 'Quick, look, there's a giant pedal car on the lake. Come and see.'

Bea stood transfixed. 'Where did it come from?'

Bilal motioned further up the beach, beyond where the bus had set us down. The land there jutted out into the lake and swept in again, out of our sight. 'There is a large hotel. It has boats and a swimming-pool.' His voice was flat and careless. 'I have worked there one summer.'

Bea and I threw ourselves at him. 'Can we go? Please? Will you take us on a pedal car?'

Bilal shook us off. I had never seen him angry before. 'You don't want that. It's rubbish. Of no use.' He kicked a half-burnt piece of wood along the beach. Bea and I followed it with longing eyes. 'Here we have everything.' He spread his arms. 'Everything in the world.'

The pedal boat began to turn slowly round and head back towards the invisible hotel.

Mum stirred under her blanket. 'Is there any tea made?'

Bilal winked at us. 'Nearly.' We helped him scrape out the white ash and rebuild the fire. The plastic bottle was still half-full. Bilal poured it into the saucepan. 'One cup each,' he said, as if it were already made.

When the water boiled he added a handful of wilting mint. Mum got up and came to sit by the fire. She had slept in her blue caftan. The caftan Ahmed's aunt had given her when she was brought back from the brink of death. It was crumpled and warm around her body. I leant against her. The sun tickled patterns of heat into my back as we sat and drank our tea and watched the fire go out.

I went with Bilal to refill our bottles from the well. I wanted to ask him about the hotel: whether you could get there by walking along the beach or whether it could only be reached by sea. He silently forbade it. Once we were out of sight of the others he hoisted me up on to his shoulders so that I could practise balancing the empty saucepan on my head. The third time Bilal had to stop and stoop for it, he didn't pass it back. We walked on in silence.

'Take hold of my hands,' he said. We had arrived at the well.

I held on.

'Now bend your head and roll.'

I sat still.

'It's a trick,' he whispered. 'A special trick.'

I held my breath and trusted him. I rolled forward, sliding into nothing. I twisted, felt myself spin round and and then with a thud I landed on the ground. Squarely on both feet. Bilal let go of my hands and clapped.

73

'Was that really a trick?'

Bilal nodded.

'Can I do it again?'

He lifted me back up. This time I kept my eyes open. Forward, turn, land. Bilal let my hands twist gently inside his, so that my arms wouldn't lock. After the fourth landing it seemed almost too easy.

'Now we must work on the speed. We must hear you whistle through the air.'

'Did I whistle that time?' I rubbed my wrists.

'Like a little mosquito.'

He threw the bucket into the well. As we waited for the hollow splash, something rustled. Bilal swung round. A young man with very blond hair and a sunburnt face greeted us in Arabic.

'Hello,' I replied.

He laughed and knelt down. 'So you're the travelling circus. I saw you from the road. I thought this man here was going to drop you down the well.' He looked up at Bilal.

'I can sing too,' I said.

'Sing? Well, you'll have to come over and sing for us.'

I wasn't sure.

'I'll give you something,' he encouraged.

'Like what?'

He thought for a while. 'A car that you wind up and then it drives along on its own?'

'All right.' I tried to contain my excitement.

'Where are you staying?' he asked.

Bilal pointed towards our particular clump of trees. 'On the Barage.'

'Charlie.' He held out his hand. 'I'll drop by.'

'My wife is English,' Bilal said as if in explanation.

I looked at him hard. I'd never heard him say 'wife' before. I wondered if they'd got married and forgotten to say.

74

'Bee-lal,' I said, drawing out the sound of his name. We were walking home hand in hand.

'Yes?'

'Am I your little girl?'

There was a long pause.

'Yes,' he said finally and he squeezed my hand very tight.

Bilal showed Bea and me how to keep water cool by tying the bottle to a stone and letting it lie floating in the lake. We took down the wall of stones around the fire and scattered the ashes away with branches, sprinkling handfuls of sand over the ground to settle the dust and make it clean and smooth again. Mum tied lengths of string between the trees and hung our bedding out to air.

'If Linda was here,' she said, 'she could have her own private washing line.'

The ground was littered with wood to be collected for that night's fire. Bilal broke the branches with his foot, stamping them into little pieces, while we dashed about bringing him new supplies.

'Right,' he said. 'Enough.'

Bea and I ran down to the lake, pulled off our clothes and slid into the water. It was cold only for a moment. We lay on our backs with everything but our faces covered and cooled, the sun forcing our eyes shut against the glare.

When I tried to speak the muddy water trickled into my mouth. 'Did you know they got married?' I said to Bea. It was half interrogation, half news.

Bea lay still beside me. 'Mum and Bilal?'

'Yes.'

'Who says?'

'Bilal told Charlie at the well.'

She rolled towards me. 'Liar!' she spat. 'You're a liar.' Her eyes had turned to stone.

'We met a man called Charlie at the well and he's going to give me a car that winds up.'

Bea kept her ears under the water and pretended not to hear.

'I promise, I promise. Cross my heart and hope to die.' I couldn't think what else to say.

We lay there for a long time. Side by side. The sun beating down through my eyelids made my head throb.

'I'm going to get a drink,' I said. But Bea wouldn't even open her eyes.

There was no one around when I got back to the camp. I rummaged through the box of food and took out two tomatoes and a piece of bread. I slid between the folds of a bedspread draped over the line. The bedspread made a cool and narrow tent. The juice from the tomato softened the bread as I chewed them together in my mouth.

I could hear voices calling my name. Voices I knew and others I didn't recognize. It was dark and the thin material flapped against me. I rolled into the open. The voices cursed and called, but I couldn't see anyone.

'I'm here,' I said. 'I'm over here.' Then I stood up and yelled. 'I'm here, I'm here, I'm HERE!'

Mum ran out through the trees. She grabbed my arm and slapped me. 'Where have you been?'

'I was asleep.' I started to cry.

She gave a long sigh and hugged me too tightly. 'We thought you'd been kidnapped or something. We even asked the shepherds to help search.'

Bilal appeared with two men. Their dogs leapt about but didn't bark. One of the shepherds whistled and the dogs slunk to the ground. Bea raised an eyebrow as she passed me. 'Hideous kinky,' she whispered and she went off to talk to the dogs.

The shepherds stayed and ate with us around the fire.

76

Under cover of darkness we fed their dogs little pieces of bread. They were big and shaggy with soft eyes that knew how to beg. Their hair was thick and matted and filthy.

'Maybe we could get them into the lake and wash them,' Bea said.

The dogs were covered in lumps like blisters that I could feel through their fur when I stroked them.

'If we give them lots of food they'll come back.'

The dogs were not fussy. They ate rice, carrots, beans, the inside of a pomegranate.

The next afternoon they were back. All three. They lay down, wagging their tails in the sand.

'Come and look.' Bea had uncovered a blister along the spine of the largest dog's back. It was dark red and swollen, fat and round as a bilberry. I touched it with my finger. The dog didn't flinch.

'Ticks,' Bilal said. He bent down. 'They suck the blood.'

'Do you mean they're alive?' I moved back involuntarily. Like body lice, but bigger, I thought.

Bilal flicked his hand through the dog's coat, uncovering whole colonies of blood-swollen ticks.

Bea was staring into the dog's mournful eyes. 'Couldn't we pull them off?'

Bilal shook his head. 'Then it is worse for the dog. If you pull them off, they leave their legs behind, and they grow again, a new body.'

We were horrified.

'The only thing to do' – Bilal took out a cigarette and lit it – 'is to burn them.'

I was sure I could hear the tick's scream as it retracted its hundred sharp legs and shrivelled into a ball, dropping grey on to the sand. The dog lay motionless, its head on its paws. It understood we were only trying to help. Bilal left us his cigarette and a box of matches. We worked through the afternoon, searching out the bloodsuckers to watch them shrivel and roll dying on to the sand. There was not time to kill each and every tick before the shepherds in the field began to whistle, and, pricking up their ears, the dogs sprang up and trotted away through the trees.

The next afternoon the dogs were back. We rewarded them with bread and chick-pea salad saved especially from lunch. Once they had eaten we set to work. There was only one dog left to do.

'We've almost finished.' I hopped around as Bea pulled, red hot, on the cigarette. I ruffled the first cured dog, stretched out asleep, his eyebrow twitching. As I stroked his matted fur, my hand caught against something, up by his neck. I fingered through and found, nestled close in to the skin, that there were fresh ticks, smaller and less swollen, but growing.

'Bilal!' I called with such urgency that he came running half naked from his siesta. 'He's got new ticks,' I sobbed, pointing at the dog.

There was nothing Bilal could say. 'When they roll in the grass, the ticks, they jump back on.'

'Don't roll in the grass,' Bea shook her finger at the dog. It wagged its tail sleepily.

Each day when the dogs came to 'scrounge' as my mother called it, we attempted to keep the ticks at bay with the cigarette-end Bea kept folded in a handkerchief especially. I secretly worried that they would never be cured. Our food supplies were running low and were most stringently watched by Mum, and without the promise of any reward I was sure the dogs would lose patience. They would lose patience, run out of blood and die.

78

CHAPTER THIRTEEN

There were fewer pedal boats on the lake, and at night it was cold enough to wrap up in a blanket and wait for supper to be ready. Mum made a soup with potatoes and a sprinkling of rice and lentils.

'Not soup again,' we moaned most nights. We bought bread from one of the shepherds' wives who baked early each morning. She gave us goat's milk in a flask which Bea and I refused to drink. There was almost nothing left in the cardboard box. No honey. No oranges. Only dried things in packets. That was why, Mum said, we should drink the milk.

One morning when I woke it was later than usual and Bilal was nowhere to be seen.

'Has he gone to the well without me?'

Mum didn't answer. She was sitting cross-legged with her back very straight. Her eyes were closed.

'She's meditating,' Bea said.

'Oh.'

'Do you remember she used to do meditating in England?'

I shook my head. On a beach? I wondered.

'Where's Bilal?'

Bea shrank her voice to a whisper in response to the angry flickering of Mum's eyelashes.

'He's gone to find some food.'

'Where from?'

'I don't know.'

Our eyes travelled in the direction of the big hotel where the water tractors moored up. We knew that it must be very far away. Twice we had set off on a secret mission to find it. We had followed the shore line, expecting the hotel to appear in all its splendour around each jut of land, but as the hours passed and the sun began to sink towards the lake, we were forced back each time without even a glimpse of it.

We waited all day for Bilal to return. We didn't even risk going in for a swim. In the afternoon when it was at its hottest we made a camp of blankets and took it in turn to keep watch. I watched for Bilal from all directions but mostly I waited for him to come from the direction of the hotel.

The sky was already turning a dusty red when I saw a small black shadow on the curve of the beach. It was Bilal. He was walking with his feet in the water. As he drew closer I saw that he had a cotton bag over one shoulder. It bulged as it swung against his hip. We ran to meet him.

'Sardines,' he shouted when he saw us, and taking out several small silver tins he began to juggle with them as he ran.

'Sardines ... and nothing else?' Mum tried not to show her disappointment.

Bilal emptied his bag. The tins poured out on to the ground like coins. There were twenty-seven of them. Twenty-seven tins of sardines. Bilal cut one open with his knife and scooped up a little silver fish. 'It's good,' he smiled, as he ate, the oil running down his chin. We dipped our fingers into the tin and broke off pieces of tightly packed fish. Rich and salty and drenched in oil. Even Mum agreed it was good.

We sat around the fire with plates of sardine chopped

80

with tomato. There was a delicious silence as we all took our first mouthful.

'Aha, so I've found you.'

A man stood just outside our circle of firelight. The flames picked out his bleached hair and the pink of his nose and cheeks.

'Hello, Charlie,' I said, my mouth full of sardine.

He stepped a little closer. He held his hand out to Mum. 'So you must be the English wife?'

Mum laughed and looked at Bilal. 'Well, not quite . . .'

Bea nudged me with a sharp elbow. 'See.'

Charlie sat and looked at our heaped plate.

'Tonight we can actually offer you something to eat,' Mum said.

Charlie smiled. 'Sardines.' He looked as if he knew what that meant. 'Thank you.'

I waited for Charlie to swallow his first mouthful before nudging him. 'Did you bring my wind-up car?'

He dug deep into the pocket of his shorts. 'Here it is.' It sat in the palm of his hand, the size of a mouse. There was a tiny key that Charlie turned until it was wound and then he let the car drive, ticking, down the length of his arm until it shot over the edge and lay, wheels spinning, in the sand. I reached for it, but Charlie closed his hand over mine.

'I thought you were going to sing me a song.'

I looked at his expectant face. Between trips to the well, collecting firewood, perfecting my one and only acrobatic trick and preserving the lives of three tick-ridden dogs, there had been no time to practise Charlie's song. I looked from the toy car to the four faces around the fire. They were all waiting. Waiting for me to sing. I struggled to my feet and closed my eyes. I didn't know any songs. I had never known any songs. All I knew was that I wanted the car. I opened my mouth and let out a low wailing chant. A poor imitation of Ahmed's tearful singing. It had

81

no beginning and no end. I added a word. An animal name from Bea's schoolbook. I half opened my eyes on Charlie's smiling mouth. I took courage and let my voice rise and fall and catch and quaver. I began to throw in some English, anything that came to mind. 'Hair grip,' I wailed. And, 'Marzipan.' Then all the sounds that seemed like songs to me flooded into my mind and I sang them. The waterman calling 'L-ma' through the city as he clanked his tin cups. The children begging in the square. 'Coca-Cola, Coca-Cola.' And the tinkling of Mrs Maynard's sweetshop door on the pantiles in Tunbridge Wells as it closed behind each customer. My song ended on a refrain of 'Helufa, Helufa, Helufa', which was met with wild applause. Charlie pressed the car into my hand.

I wound it carefully and set it on the ground. Its wheels spun against the pine needles and pebbles, but it moved an inch or two. I thought of the long, smooth terrace of the Hotel Moulay Idriss. 'Thank you,' I said and knotted it tightly into the hem of my caftan.

CHAPTER FOURTEEN

There were still five tins of sardines left when Bea and I took them to the edge of the Barage and threw them in.

'What are we going to do now?' I asked her, peering into the empty cardboard box. Mum and Bilal were sleeping in the washing-line tent. It was mid-afternoon. 'We could visit Charlie,' I suggested. 'I think he lives somewhere near the well.'

We crept away through the trees. The dogs followed, across the road and towards the well. We had given up trying to cure them of ticks and it was days since there had been any food to spare, but they still came diligently to visit every afternoon. We sat by the well and waited aimlessly for Charlie to appear.

'Have we been here for a very long time?' I asked Bea.

'Where?'

'At the Barage.'

'I think so.' She splashed her face with water from the plastic bucket.

'When we go back, will you go to school again?'

'I might do,' she said.

'What do you want most in the whole world?'

Bea closed her eyes. Little drops of water glistened on her eyelids. 'Mashed potato ...' she said, 'and a Mars Bar.'

I threw sticks for the dogs. They lay on their sides and

let the flies settle on the black skin of their smiles. 'Fetch. Good dog. Fetch.' They looked at me with sleepy eyes.

'They're not stupid,' Bea said.

I leant down for another stick. Something rustled by my hand. I pulled away to see a scorpion, furious, trembling on its ice-thin, razor-sharp legs, scuttle towards me. It had poison in its tail, and its arms were whips of iron. 'One sting from a scorpion and you could be dead within three hours.' That's what I'd heard. 'If you don't get to a hospital within the first hour ...' I was paralysed with fear. What if there weren't any hospitals on the Barage? I was waiting for the sliver of scorpion to dart through the slits in my plastic sandal. It glided over the ground like a streak of lightning and at the last moment disappeared under a stone.

I fought for air. 'Did you see it?'

'What? See what?'

'A scorpion.' I pointed, my hands still trembling.

'It was probably a lizard.' Bea took a stick and went to prise up the stone.

'Don't,' I pleaded. 'Please don't.'

'Stand behind me,' she ordered. 'And if it comes out, we'll run.'

I thought about the man who visited us in the Mellah. He let six scorpions run over his hands like water. Then he put them back in their box and asked for money. Mum said he must have done something to them, taken out their sting or something, but she gave him money anyway. The scorpion man. Once I found a dead scorpion in the garden and Akari crushed it between two stones and left it on our doorstep. 'It will be a warning to all scorpions,' he said, 'not to enter this house.' Like a magic spell.

Bea tipped the stone over. As it fell away, a swarming nest spilt out of the hollow and spread over the ground like a sheet of fire, tails flailing in the light. Bea pulled at my hand and we ran. Our feet barely skimming the ground

84

and my heart beating loud enough to burst my ears. We ran through the field of sheep and out on to the road. We ran until we could no longer see the well. When we stopped running I had a stitch, and I remembered we'd left the dogs behind. Bea put her fingers in her mouth and whistled but they didn't come.

We set off again at a marching pace. 'Left, left, left my wife and five fat children.' I copied Bea, swinging my arms. 'Right, right, right in the middle of the kitchen floor.' We marched on and on, hopping from one foot to the other at the end of each stanza until our breathing was low and calm again.

We turned off the road and cut back to the edge of the Barage. There was no beach at this point, just a ridge of rock where the water swirled and tumbled as it pulled away with each wave. We sat on the edge and threw stones into the water. There was something comforting about the sound they made as they hit the surface and disappeared. We watched the sun hanging just above the water and tried to catch it moving. At times it seemed to stay exactly still and it was the lake that rose up to engulf it.

By the time we started for home the sky was striped with gold and pink and green and we knew that in a moment it would be dark. Bea told me 'Missee Piggin and the Forty Thieves'. 'Missee Piggin' was a story Bea had made up about me. I was Missee Piggin and Bea, there had never been any doubt, was the Forty Thieves.

Mum held us just above the elbow and shook us. 'Where have you been?'

I could see her teeth flash in the dark. The silver bracelets she wore on her arm were digging into my flesh. All I could think of was the nest of scorpions and that was hours and hours ago.

'A man followed us with a knife,' Bea said in a terrifying

whisper. Mum loosened her grip.

'We hid until it was dark. We hid behind a tree.'

Mum rocked backwards on her heels. 'My God!' she said, and she hugged us both so tight I could hardly breathe. 'Please, please, don't wander off on your own again.' She turned to Bea and looked at her straight in the face. 'I'm going to tell you this because you're the eldest.' Her voice was low and serious. 'There are people out there who are dangerous. This time you've been lucky, but I want you to promise me to be careful.'

'I promise,' Bea said, very solemnly.

'I promise too,' I vowed, unasked.

CHAPTER FIFTEEN

We could hear Mob's familiar cry as we trudged up the dusty, tiled steps of the Hotel Moulay Idriss. There was no one in the courtyard or on the terrace but the air was full of steaming couscous and the smell of chopped coriander. Low murmurings and the clinking of glasses drifted out through open doorways. In our room something was burning. Linda was bending over the mijmar and the room was full of smoke.

'Thank God you're back.' She was close to tears as she greeted us. 'I've been so worried.'

Mob's screams rose above the commotion. Mum picked her up and laughed in surprise. 'And what's happened to you?' She said, bouncing her in her arms.

'We ran out of powdered baby food.' Linda indicated Mob's changed appearance. 'And she doesn't seem to like anything else.'

Mob was no longer the solid pink baby she had been. She had transformed into a thin brown child with only the same puzzled eyes to know her by.

'Also . . .' Linda sat down lumpily on a mattress. 'We've run out of money.'

'What about your job?'

'There turned out to only be ten poems in his head. So there was nothing else for me to type.'

'Surely he could have thought up some more?'

'That's what I kept saying.' Mum and Linda began to giggle. 'But apparently not.'

Mum collected her letters from the Post Office and the money that had arrived at the bank, and we all went to eat at our old café in the Djemaa El Fna. The waiter, the cook and the manager all welcomed us as if we had been away for ever, and we took a table right on the edge of the square, half in and half out of the shade.

Mum was wearing her Biba dress and her eyes sparkled. 'Whatever you want for lunch,' she announced.

'Fanta please,' I sang every time the waiter passed. 'Fanta please.'

We ate Moroccan salad and a plate of chicken tajine that was almost the size of the table and arrived with its flowerpot hat on.

As we ate Mum looked through her letters. 'My mother is praying that we'll all be home safe and sound for Christmas,' she read.

'Christmas? Do you get Christmas here?'

'And she hopes the children are looking after their teeth.' She frowned. Our one tube of toothpaste had run out in the first few weeks of spring in the Mellah. My Fanta gurgled through its straw.

'John and Maretta are having a baby.' She turned to Linda.

'A baby? Haven't they got one already, a little girl?'

'Yes.' My mother lowered her voice. 'But she was taken into care.'

Linda sighed. 'I remember now.'

'What's care?'

Mum folded up the letter and slipped it into its envelope. 'And that's enough Fanta for one day,' she said.

'Now Mob isn't so heavy, can I carry her on my back?' Bea asked quickly, gulping down the remainder of her bottle before any more serious ban could be declared.

Linda shook out her shawl and strapped Mob on, tight across Bea's back. 'Don't go too far,' she shouted after us as we slipped off into the crowd to find Khadija and the beggar girls who roamed the square.

We stopped to watch the Gnaoua as they danced like Russians to their brass clackers and drums. Mob stared transfixed over Bea's shoulder as the men squatted and kicked out their legs.

'It's the Fool,' Bea whispered, pointing to a dirty and dishevelled man dancing wildly on the fringes of the group. 'I've seen him before.'

As we watched, the Fool took a particularly abandoned leap, tripped, and landed on his back, ripping his thread-bare djellaba so that it fell away and left him stretched out naked on the ground. The crowd tittered. The Fool picked himself up and, with a moment to fasten his cloak, worked himself back into the dance.

When the music stopped, the Gnaoua offered him a drink. He grinned, dribbling at his new friends, and tried to clasp them in his arms. They smiled down on him, tall and gentle and shimmering blue-black against his dusty face.

The drummer girls called to us as we passed. 'Waa, waa.' They leapt up from their display of painted drums and surrounded us, flapping like butterflies in their brightly coloured caftans. They unstrapped Mob and carried her off to crawl among their rows of drums while they tapped out tunes for her on the tight skin tops. The drummer girls had lengths of braid plaited into their oiled hair and mostly their earrings were a loop of plastic wire hung with beads. They pressed the drums we admired into our hands and before we had a chance to refuse, Mob had smashed hers on the cobbles and was cramming the pieces of broken clay into her mouth. One of the girls who had a baby of her own shook Mob till her hands and

89

mouth were empty and helped to restrap her on to Bea's back. I caught Bea's eye as we moved away.

'They are forever giving the children things,' Mum had despaired to Linda, 'and they must be so poor.'

'Poorer than Khadija's mother?' I had asked.

But she had gone on mumbling. 'Nothing, they have nothing, and they give the drums away . . .' As if she could unravel the mystery with words.

Clutching our drums we passed among the stalls of fruit. Water melons, oranges, prickly pears that were too dangerous to eat. We passed the women at the mouth of the market who sat like sentries in their high boxes with bread for sale. Some sold round white loaves, and others black. An old lady squatted by a pile of six oranges and while we watched she sold one, taking the coins and stowing them carefully away inside her djellaba, before settling back to wait patiently by her five remaining oranges for the next customer to pass.

'What do you think happens if nothing gets sold?' I asked Bea as we passed a man dozing in front of a box of peppers.

'They just eat them,' she said.

Khadija, Zara and Saida were engrossed in tormenting a tourist. 'Tourist, tourist,' they chanted. We watched as a man bought a cup of water from the waterman and a woman in a blue dress stood back to take a photograph. 'Tourist, tourist.' They held out their hands.

'Tourist,' I muttered under my breath, but my newly washed trousers with Bilal's patch blazing on the knee stopped me from joining in.

'Waa Khadija.' We called them. 'Waa Saida, Waa waa Zara.' And they ran over to us, leaving the couple to wander unchaperoned back to their hotel. We squatted in a circle to exchange news. Mob stared into the black eyes of Khadija's baby sister as her head bobbed against Bea's shoulder. Saida inspected Bilal's patch. Saida was smaller than me and thin with big black eyes and straight shiny hair. She began to pick at the patch with her fingers and then when it wouldn't come loose she held out her hand for it. I looked at her, my mouth dry, and shook my head so violently she pulled away.

That evening as I sat on Bilal's knee begging a scrape of majoun, I asked, 'Can I keep my trousers and just wear them when we live in England?'

'If they still fit you,' Bea said.

'Yes, of course,' Mum agreed and ordered another pot of mint tea.

The square was lit with the lights of a hundred stalls of food. They appeared at sunset and were set out in lanes through which you could wander and choose where to eat your supper. There were stalls decorated with the heads of sheep where meat kebabs grilled on spits, and others that sold snails that you picked out of their shells with a piece of wire. There were cauldrons of harira – a soup that was only on sale in the evening – and whole stalls devoted to fried fish, and others that sold chopped spinach soaked in oil and covered in olives like a pie. Each stall had a tilley lamp or two which they pumped to keep the bulbs burning and metal benches on three sides where you could sit and eat. Single women crouched in the reflected light of this maze of restaurants and sold eggs from under their skirts.

I leant against Bilal's shoulder. 'When we do live in England,' I continued, my mind on another life, 'will you be coming too?'

Bilal closed his eyes and began to hum along with Om Kalsoum, whose voice crackled and wept through a radio in the back of the café.

'Tomorrow,' Mum said eventually, when the song had cried itself out, 'Bilal will be starting his work with the Hadaoui.'

'Here? In the Djemaa El Fna?'

'Yes, for a day or two. And then in other places.'

'In Casablanca?'

'Yes, and others.'

'Can I be the flower girl?'

Bilal nodded, his eyes still closed.

'And Bea? Can she be a flower girl too?'

'I might be at school,' Bea said. 'Tomorrow,' she announced, sitting up very straight, 'I am going back to school.'

'But are your things ready?' Mum asked doubtfully.

'Yes,' she said, 'I washed them this afternoon. They're hanging out to dry.'

'That's if they haven't been stolen,' Linda muttered.

CHAPTER SIXTEEN

Bea disappeared down the steps of the Hotel Moulay Idriss, hand in hand with Ayesha. The Henna Ladies had no use for her white uniform. They walked around the terrace and ran their fingers through my hair that now hung halfway down my back. They sat and talked with Mob and me on the doorstep while Mum did her morning's meditation and Linda stayed inside and continued to declare war. I wished the Henna Ladies would come to the Djemaa El Fna to see Bilal working his Hadaoui magic with the crowd, but they never left the hotel. They stayed on their landing, lounging in worn-down babouches and wearing their caftans like nighties with their hair loose. They had friends who would visit them, men who disappeared into the thick perfumed stillness of their double rooms and sometimes sat through whole afternoons on their cushioned doorstep to smoke and drink tea while the Henna Ladies smiled serenely over them like the proudest of mothers.

'You notice they don't steal when there's a man in the house,' Linda said. It was the morning after Bilal had left with the Hadaoui and another nappy was missing.

For a week of afternoons the Hadaoui had performed in the square to an enormous crowd. Everyone came to watch. Akari the Estate Agent, Moulay Idriss, the drummer girls, various members of the Gnaoua and the Fool. Even Bea finished school in time.

Khadija and I watched the Hadaoui as he sat quite still in the middle of his carpet, his purple turban nodding as he blew bubbles of smoke out of his pipe. We hovered on the carpet's edge and waited for our moment. Bilal having lifted each dove out of its box, began to shoulder his way through the crowd, heckling and calling until finally the Hadaoui lifted up his head and cried 'Umwi, Umwi', making the people roar with laughter to see such an old man calling for his Mummy.

'Umwi, Umwi.' I tried to attract my mother's attention, but she was talking to one of the Gnaoua wives and she wouldn't look round.

The Gnaoua wives, like the men, were tall and thin. They kept their faces covered with a veil. The lady Mum was talking to looked just like the other wives, but as she stood with her back to me I noticed that the long wrists and delicate hands that hung from the sleeves of her caftan were white. A Gnaoua lady with white hands! I tried to point her out to Khadija, but she wouldn't take her eyes off the Hadaoui.

'Umwi, Umwi, Mum...' I called again, hoping the Gnaoua lady would turn around, but they carried on talking and Kahdija tugged at my arm to draw my attention back to the show. The Fool had begun to follow Bilal, mimicking him and snorting with laughter whenever Bilal spoke, but always remaining watchful not to let his feet disrespectfully cross over on to the tasselled edges of the carpet. The Hadaoui continued to smoke and roll his eyes. 'Umwi, Umwi,' he sighed from time to time and shook his head. Eventually he stood up and entered into a heated discussion with Bilal which I could not follow, but which made Khadija rock on her heels as she giggled and her usually solemn face light up. I squatted next to her and held my breath for the show to be over, counting the

94

minutes before it was my turn to cross over on to the Hadaoui's magic carpet.

Now Bilal was on his way to Casablanca and Bea was at school. Even Linda was talking about going back to London. She had received a letter from her mother, who had not only discovered where she was but that she had had a baby.

'She's our only grandchild,' Linda read aloud, 'she must be nearly a year old, and we don't even know her name.'

Mum and Linda laughed so hard that I had to pat their backs to stop them choking.

'Well, my mother still wouldn't know,' Mum said when she had recovered, 'except a friend of hers saw me waiting at a bus stop in Camden Town with a baby in a pushchair and Bea who was nearly three. "I didn't know your daughter was married," she said to her when they next met.' Mum wiped her eyes. 'I'd have given a lot to have seen her face.'

Linda had been persuaded to stay until after Christmas.

'Will we have a stocking?' I looked around anxiously, realizing for the first time there were no chimneys in the Hotel Moulay Idriss.

'I'm sure Father Christmas will think of something,' Mum assured me.

Last Christmas we hung up a pair of Mum's long socks. A sock each. This year she didn't have any socks. She hadn't packed any. I thought about our Christmas tree all glittering with tinsel and wondered if it was still standing on the front lawn where we'd planted it, its cut-out golden angel on top. Bea and I had waved at it through the back windows of John's van as we drove away. I sat on the doorstep while Mum meditated and Linda counted nappies, and tried to remember all the things and people and places Bea and I had waved at.

*

'Would you like to visit Luna and Umbark?' Mum sat down beside me on the step. We could hear Linda hissing inside the room. '. . . five, six . . . Aha! . . . I knew there were eight of those. One . . . two . . . Damn.'

Luna was the lady with the white hands. She was married to Umbark who was a dancer with the Gnaoua. Luna was from Denmark. We had sat with them the evening before at a table in the outside café waiting for the sun to set. Until the sun set we were not allowed to eat or even drink Fanta because it was the first day of Ramadan.

'What is Ramadan?' I asked.

'It's a Muslim festival. For twenty-eight days you mustn't eat, drink or smoke between the hours of sunrise and sunset and for a month no one must have sex.'

'What's sex?'

Linda started to explain, but Mum quieted her so we could listen to Luna's story.

Luna had come to Morocco three years before. 'Looking for some fun times and adventure.' She nodded at Mum from under her veil. 'But then I met Umbark.' She had met Umbark soon after she arrived in Morocco and they had fallen in love.

Umbark sat silently by and listened to Luna's story. He was as tall and thin and black as Luna was tall and thin and white. Twins from a fairy tale. Since their marriage Luna lived her life as a strict Muslim woman. She even stayed at home in Marrakech when Umbark travelled to Germany in the summer months to work as part of a human pyramid in the circus. By the time Luna finished her story the sun had almost set. The tables in our café and in the other cafés in the square were fast filling up and the waiters rushed about placing steaming bowls of harira in front of each customer.

'It is traditional to break the fast each evening with a bowl of this soup,' Luna told us.

So we ordered our harira and sat staring at it, waiting for night to officially descend. A silence settled over the square. Then as the sky turned red behind the Koutoubia a siren rang out and lamps were lit in the minarets of every mosque. The swollen voice of a holy man chanted the day's end from the top tower, his voice drifting in and out of the breeze, and as the prayer tailed away a calm settled over the city.

CHAPTER SEVENTEEN

Luna and Umbark lived in one small room in a street in the Mellah not far from our old house. Luna opened the door to us dressed in a plain white caftan and without her veil. Her face was round and golden white and her blue eyes watered when she smiled.

'Come in, come in,' she said, leaning down to kiss me.

There was nothing in the room except a mattress covered in woven rugs and a mijmar on which an iron pot bubbled and stewed, giving out the delicious smell of tajine.

'Please, I am not expecting you to fast also.' Luna glanced at the pot. 'So I have made something for your lunch.'

Mum's colour rose. 'I should have told you, during Ramadan, I think ... I have decided, I am also going to fast.'

'And pray?'

Mum paused. 'Yes, and pray. In fact I am very interested ... how shall I say it? I want to become a Sufi.'

'Does that mean I won't be allowed to have lunch either?' I wanted to know.

'The Sufis do not pray five times a day like us,' Luna warned, 'they pray seven times.'

Luna set down a tray of tiny honey-filled pastries in front of me.

'Where's Umbark?' I asked her.

'He was called out to a woman who is sick.'

'Is Umbark a doctor?'

'All the Gnaoua have special healing powers that have been passed down through each generation,' Luna said proudly. 'They stay by the side of the sick and pray and play their drums. They burn incense in the mijmar until the sick one goes into a trance and then they beat the devil out.'

'How long does it take?' I crammed a pastry into my mouth.

'That is never the same. Sometimes a few hours and sometimes days and days.'

'And do they see the devil actually coming out?'

'No, they just see the sick one becoming well again.'

'Even if you get bitten by a scorpion?'

'Especially if you get bitten by a scorpion. The Gnaoua have magic powers to draw the poison out.'

I wanted to ask more questions about scorpion bites and if there was a cure for dog ticks and whether or not you could die from body lice, but Mum wanted to talk to Luna about the Sufi. Luna said that Sufi was the unorthodox side of Islam. The mystical side.

'During Ramadan the Sufis begin their prayers, like us, at sunset. They pray after dark, at sunrise, at midday, mid-afternoon and then again at sunset. And' – Luna screwed up her eyes in concentration – 'they perform a ritual washing of nose, ears and arms before each prayer and it is important to remove your shoes.'

'Oh Mum, please...' I was prepared to beg. 'Please don't be a Sufi.'

Mum took me with her when she went to buy her prayer mat. There were thousands to choose from, packed so tightly in multicoloured columns of wool that it seemed impossible to choose one without disturbing a whole tower.

Mum was dressed in her haik, pulled halfway across her face for the occasion. As we passed down the lanes of carpet, the stallholders called to us, sliding the rugs expertly out and holding them up for our inspection.

She chose a small wool mat. 'So I can take it with me when I go out,' she said.

I wanted her to choose a thick woven carpet, too heavy to leave the house.

'Children are always embarrassed by their mothers.' She guessed the reason for my dragging feet. She held the mat rolled like a scroll under her arm. 'My mother used to put her lipstick on on the top deck of the bus.'

I kicked against the road as we walked and continued to resist the warm fingers of her hand as they reached for mine.

For weeks the city was calm and quiet and hungry during the day, but each evening once the prayers from the mosque had faded into night a party broke out. Mum was keen to abide by the rules of Ramadan, and she rose at dawn, washed, prayed, and got back into bed. Sometimes I would wake to hear her mumbling a mantra of long vowels, a little like the song I had sung for Charlie on the Barage, and that usually succeeded in lulling me to sleep again.

Mum managed to persuade Linda to join her in her fast, but as far as praying was concerned Linda said it was bad enough being on a diet that didn't make you any thinner, without having to get up at the crack of dawn to mumble words you didn't even understand. Bea, Mob and I were allowed to eat and drink whatever we liked as long as we did it behind closed doors.

Mum looked on with a scornful smile as Linda spooned apple purée into Mob's open mouth. 'One for you and one for . . . me. One for you and one for . . . MUMMY.'

'It's not eating,' Linda said defiantly, 'it's just encouragement.'

At night Mum broke her fast with a bowl of harira at a café in the Djemaa El Fna. We sat up late into the night drinking syrupy mint tea and talking to the people who drew chairs up at our table: men from the Gnaoua we had come to know through Umbark, Linda's blind poet who would occasionally appear, and Akari the Estate Agent, always in a bustle of excitement over what he called his 'business', and who would inevitably greet us with detailed reports of Snowy, our old black hen and stories of her seven newly hatched chicks.

'Do you think she'd remember us if we came to visit?' Bea asked him after a story which involved Snowy rescuing his youngest child from a dog.

Akari clapped his hands and turned hurriedly away to tell Mum about an outside cinema he had just built in his home village. Our darkest suspicions were confirmed.

'Snowy's been eaten,' Bea proclaimed and she made me promise not to talk to Akari ever again.

Bea and I left Mum drinking tea and nibbling on a lump of majoun and wandered off to play games in the square. Hideous kinky tag was still our favourite, and we kept a good eye out for Luigi Mancini at all times.

Mob was usually too sleepy even to be carried and Linda would wrap her in a blanket and lay her under the table. On nights when my eyes began to swim and my legs shiver with the cold, I draped myself in Mum's burnous and, using the hood as a pillow, crawled down beside her.

One night as we stumbled home, me moaning on my mother's hand to be carried, we found that we were being followed. A man trailed us through the streets, the shadow of his peaked hood looming darkly against the walls of houses. We hurried on, our ears sharp and listening for the flapping of the man's babouches as they kept a steady pace with ours. Mum gripped my hand, and Mob was hoisted on to Linda's other hip. Bea's skipping walk became a run as she twisted in her tracks to check our chances of escape. I flew on my mother's hand, my fingers white in hers, the toes of my sandals sparking as they grazed the road.

Breathless, we reached the tall doors of the hotel and as we slid through into the safety of the courtyard, Bea stopped and called out, 'Look, it's only the Fool.'

'It's the Fool, it's the Fool,' I repeated in a swirl of relief and the Fool bowed his head and raised his hands in a greeting.

The Fool became our private escort, following us home if we stayed out after dark, so that soon we were so accustomed to his silent presence we wondered how we'd ever dared go anywhere alone.

Bea continued to go to school. She knew the name for every picture in her book, even the words for lampshade, wheelbarrow, and a plaster cast for when you break your arm.

'I'll never be allowed to go to school,' I said, watching as Bea skirted the edge of the playground. There was a fight between two boys from the school next door and a third, who stood on the outside kicking the one who was losing. He was kicking him in the back of the knees. Bea dodged the fight and arrived at the gate where Mum and I were waiting.

'How was it today?' Mum asked.

'All right.' Bea swung the cotton sardine bag she still used as a satchel.

We followed her out into the street.

'But I won't ever, will I? Will I?' I insisted on an answer.

'What?'

'Be allowed to go to school?'

'Not quite yet,' Mum said to my secret relief, but I persisted anyway.

'But when then?'

'When you're a little older.'

'When will that be?'

'I don't know at the moment.' She was losing patience.

'Never,' I muttered under my breath.

I thought about the boy with the stick and the girl who was too frightened to ask to go to the toilet. Never, I decided. Then I began to worry about how if we ever did go home I wouldn't know anything. Not how to read. Or write my name. Or tell the time. Or anything.

Bea and I were eager to arrive at the hotel before Mum's next prayers were due. A few days before, on our way back from the flea market by the old gate of the city, Mum had stopped abruptly, looked up at the sun and, unperturbed by the fact that she had forgotten her prayer mat, knelt down in the street to pray. She mimed her intricate washing procedures and stretched out her arms to Mecca. Without a word we hid ourselves behind a wall. We agreed firmly that, if asked, we'd never seen or heard of her before. From time to time we peered cautiously out, only to see the same straggly bunch of children watching from a distance and the occasional trader slow down his laden donkey to throw her a quizzical look. I told Bea about Mum's mother putting lipstick on on the top of a bus, and she agreed with me that it didn't sound such a terrible thing to do.

'She didn't know how lucky she was,' she said.

Finally Mum stood up and dusted down her clothes. We crept out from behind our wall and, punishing her with a vow of silence, kept our distance on the journey home.

CHAPTER EIGHTEEN

It was a drizzly, warm grey afternoon when we met Aunty Rose. Bea and I were carrying fruit home from the market, and I was in the middle of a story about two sisters who get adopted by a kind old man in silver-and-gold waistcoats, when we were stopped short by a large, laughing lady in a flowery dress.

'And where are you off to in such a hurry?' she said, looking into our basket of oranges. 'Not running away, I hope?'

Her voice was happy at the end of every sentence and she talked as if she had known us for a long time. Her round cheeks were crossed with tiny pink lines that wrinkled up when she smiled and her soft, grey hair was piled high over her head and held in place by a multitude of pins.

'Well and I haven't even introduced myself,' she said, placing her hands firmly on her hips and smiling. 'Rose. But to you' – she fixed us with a tiny frown – 'Aunty Rose.'

'Aunty Rose,' we both mumbled obediently.

'And now, I think you should both come back to my house and we'll have a glass of lemonade.'

'We could have a biscuit too,' I added quickly, 'because Mum says we don't have to fast if we don't want to.'

Bea kicked me.

Aunty Rose took my hand and said 'I should think not

too' very indignantly and she marched us off down the street.

Aunty Rose lived in a house that had shrunk. It must once have been on the same level as the street, but now you had to climb down two steep steps to go through the front door. Aunty Rose bent her head and stooped low as she unlocked the door with an iron key, only straightening up once she was inside. All the rooms were white and small and the windows were arches through which you could see people's legs up to the knee hurrying past in the courtyard outside.

Aunty Rose had furniture. In our house everything was on the floor but Aunty Rose had a wooden bed with legs and a table at which you could sit on high-backed chairs. There was a checked cloth on the table and a jug of yellow roses.

She made lemonade with white sugar and lemon juice. She poured us each a glass with a green sprig of mint floating on the top and set down a plate of wafer-thin biscuits. The biscuits tasted of almonds and melted in your mouth.

'You never know when you're going to have company,' Aunty Rose smiled, smoothing her dress over her lap. She took a long drink of lemonade and asked, 'Excited about tomorrow?'

We looked at her. 'Tomorrow?'

'Good grief, girls,' Aunty Rose snorted with amusement, and then, softening, as if moved to pity by our state of ignorance said gently, 'Christmas.'

'Christmas? Tomorrow?'

We were stunned.

'Cross your heart and hope to die,' I tried to make her swear.

'What . . . Christmas when Father Christmas comes?'

'How do you know for definite?'

'When you hang up stockings?'

'But we haven't even got a present for Mum.' Bea was worried.

Aunty Rose convinced us with her tree in a bucket in the corner of the sitting-room. It was a baby pine with no decoration. By its side were arranged small clay figures and a brown clay cradle with a cow. 'Mary, Joseph and the baby Jesus,' Aunty Rose explained. 'I made them myself.'

I would have liked to stay and learn how to make things out of clay, especially the animals, but Bea was in a sudden hurry to be gone. Aunty Rose packed up the remaining biscuits and gave them to Bea to carry. 'I'll only eat them otherwise,' she said, patting her stomach. She made us promise to visit her again so that we could collect our Christmas presents.

'She didn't say "present",' I pointed out to Bea once we were outside, 'she said "presents".'

Bea was preoccupied. 'What are we going to get for Mum?'

All I could think of was a clay drum.

'A clay drum?' I suggested.

'No.'

Hard as I tried I couldn't think of anything else. We walked in silence through the streets away from Aunty Rose's house, surreptitiously eating biscuits and trying to avoid the swishing tail of a donkey that was walking just in front. In the Djemaa El Fna we searched for anything that might transform itself into a possible present for our mother. There were Berber women selling bracelets with blue stones and a man from the mountains with a cloth covered in pendants of carved amethyst.

Bea counted our money. It was the money left over from shopping. Thirty-five centimes. We looked at the spice stalls and the loaves of black bread, the water melons, the pomegranates and potatoes, the almonds and peanuts in their shells, the pumpkin seeds, pistachios and chickpeas. Then I saw it. A stall that had never been there before. A stall of ripe, red strawberries.

'Strawberries!' Bea's voice was a whisper of admiration.

The strawberries were sold in wicker cornets. A cornet cost fifty centimes. Bea asked if we could buy half a cornet but the man said no. She tried to swop two oranges to make up the extra fifteen centimes but the strawberry man wasn't interested. We gazed longingly at the strawberries for nearly half an hour, hoping to be taken pity on. Eventually we gave up.

As we walked despondently away through the square we saw the same woman as before dozing by her pile of oranges.

'Come on.' Bea pulled me towards her. A row of people squatted by their makeshift stalls. 'Come on.'

We arranged our six oranges, carefully balancing them into a pyramid, and when we were satisfied with the display we sat proudly back and waited. Waited for business to begin. Bea said that if we sold each orange for five centimes we'd only have to sell three oranges to have enough money to buy the strawberries.

We made bets on the passers-by. 'I bet the fifth woman who passes will stop and buy . . .'

'What?'

'Three oranges.'

When the fifth woman hurried past, eyes averted, we started again.

'I bet . . .'

We'd been playing this game for what seemed like a very long time when we realized the fifth woman walking directly towards us was Mum. She was approaching too fast for us to get up, pack up our oranges and run, so we bent our heads, letting our hair hang down over our faces, and pretended to be deep in conversation. Bea in Arabic, me in the language I had perfected for the singing of my songs – something I now used as a way of acquiring otherwise unobtainable possessions. Mum's ankles swished under her haik as she passed just feet in front of us. She passed our stall and strode purposefully on, stopping only to buy a loaf of bread. Then she rounded a corner and disappeared into the maze of narrow streets that led away from the square.

We were so busy discussing our triumph of disguise that it took some time to realize we had a customer. It was the Fool. He had on a new djellaba, and since he danced with the Gnaoua every afternoon and was their friend he also wore something underneath. He bought one orange. Bea let him have it for four centimes. He sat with us while he ate it, sucking the juice out through a hole he made with his thumb. He only had one tooth. It was brown and pointed and was right at the side of his mouth. Bea asked him what had happened to his other teeth, but he shook his head and said he never had any other teeth. 'Just this one, only ever this one.'

The Fool was still sucking on his orange when a woman stopped and began to barter. She wanted to give us ten centimes for four oranges. Bea refused to sell unless we got twenty. Finally a deal was struck: four oranges for fifteen centimes. When she had gone, we peeled the remaining orange and split it three ways before going off to buy our strawberries.

Convinced that I'd never really been asleep I woke at dawn to inspect my stocking, which was in fact one of Linda's babouches with the heel flattened down. I had chosen Linda's shoe because Linda had the biggest feet. It was dark in the room and I had to search silently with my hands for the shoes which we'd left propped up near the door for Father Christmas. I needn't have worried so much about there not being a chimney, because as my eyes became accustomed to the dark I saw that the babouche had been filled.

'Bea.' I shook her awake. 'He's been.'

I wanted to tell her that there was a long, thin packet of something in the shoe that smelt of rose petals, but I knew she'd be angry if I ruined any element of her surprise. She jumped out of bed and ran to open the door. Maybe she was hoping to catch a last glimpse of Father Christmas as he disappeared down the steps by the toilet in his red coat with the white fur edging. Through the open door the morning filtered in in pale green banana-leaf-shaped patterns and buzzed with the chatter of waking birds, stretching their wings in the courtyard. The occasional crow of a cock hung mournfully across the roofs.

Bea brought her babouche back to bed. I waited for her. I had learnt to be wary of Bea on occasions like this. The year before in Tunbridge Wells she had forced me to creep under the Christmas tree and unwrap my present, just enough to see inside, and then the next day I had to pretend to be surprised and delighted at a jigsaw puzzle I already knew turned into a picture of a train.

Bea began to unwrap her package. There was something familiar about the cone-shaped wicker basket protruding from the shoe. It was full of soft fruit that spilt on to the sheet when I tipped it up.

'Stawberries!' we both shouted, waking Mob who began to scream. Mum stirred under her blanket and eventually got up to pray.

'Thank you. How lovely,' she said, when presented with her present. 'Mulberries.'

'Mulberries!' We were devastated.

Mum tried to check our disappointment. 'They're exactly the same as strawberries only more delicious and much, much rarer.' Bea gave her a look usually reserved for Akari the Estate Agent, but as it was Christmas we decided to let it go. We sat up in bed and ate our mulberries. Mob also had a carton, and Mum let Linda eat half of hers.

'The sun's only just risen,' Linda said, eating guiltily, 'and after all it is Christmas.'

Mum saved her share for later.

She said there was a surprise for us. She made us close our eyes. My heart leapt. Bilal. It had to be Bilal. I could see him in my mind's eye juggling with sardines and Christmas presents, somersaulting across the room.

'All right, you can open your eyes now,' Mum's voice came from far away.

Bea gave me a shove. 'Open your eyes.'

In the centre of the room was a large brown parcel. It was wound round and round with Sellotape and covered in stamps. Mum cut at it with a knife. We pulled and scratched until finally one of its cardboard sides came away and a white paper bag of Liquorice Laces fell out. There were Sherbet Fountains, Black Jacks, Midget Gems, Gobstoppers, Flying Saucers, but the real present was three tall books with pictures of animals on the front. *Orlando the Marmalade Cat, Babar the Elephant* and a Rupert Bear book. Bea and I began to devour the sweets.

'Don't you want to know who they're from?' Mum asked as we ripped off wrappings, spraying the room with sherbet.

'Your Daddy,' she said. 'From England.'

My teeth were stuck together with Black Jack. I opened up *Babar the Elephant*. I wondered if he was there with Luigi Mancini or not. Bea didn't say anything. She started to explain to me about Orlando and his magic carpet. She showed me a picture of Orlando's wife, Grace, and their three children, Pansy, Blanche and Tom the kitten. I pored over the pictures, forcing her to tell me the names of each new character. For a while I forgot about Bilal and the mystery man in waistcoats who magicked sweets out of a cardboard box, falling in and out of love with

Grace in her elegant hats, Rupert's friend Bill the Badger, and Babar's three children, Flora, Alexander and Pom.

CHAPTER NINETEEN

Linda was leaving for London. Bea and I insisted on wearing our pyjamas to see her off. They were the pyjamas Aunty Rose had given us on Boxing Day. After all, we were only waving goodbye to the bus that goes to the airport and not to the plane.

A terrible mistake had been made over the pyjamas. One pair was pale blue and obviously meant for Bea, the other, smaller pair were the colour of honeycomb and scattered with teddy bears, running, jumping and standing on their heads. I reached eagerly for them, but Aunty Rose stopped me, saying, 'Bea, seeing as you're the eldest would you like to choose which pyjamas you'd prefer?'

I stood still, willing her under my breath, 'The blue ones, the blue ones,' until I saw Bea slip her caftan over her head and take up the wrong pair. The trousers hung high above her ankles and the sleeves were ridiculously short. She buttoned up the shirt and beamed. 'I'll take these.'

She even said, 'Thank you.'

Aunty Rose dressed me in the blue pyjamas. She tied the cord across my stomach in a bow, and turned the sleeves over three times. I kept expecting her to notice something was wrong, but she hummed contentedly and knelt to roll up the trouser legs.

We wore our pyjamas home. Mum admired them

without criticism, only advising us to take them off before getting into bed.

We stood at the bus station and waved goodbye to Linda and Mob. Linda was crying and Mob was scrambling about all over the seat. 'Take care of yourselves,' she kept saying.

The bus began to pull away. 'Good luck!' Mum shouted, and Linda waved one of Mob's nappies out of the back window to make us laugh.

Ramadan was over and Mum was allowed to eat with us again. No one could think of anything to say as we waited for our soup to cool. I volunteered a song to cheer Mum up, but for once she was unenthusiastic. She bought a piece of majoun and began to chew it slowly. I wondered if now that Linda and Mob had gone away Bilal would come back. Each time I went to ask about him the words stopped in my mouth. A distant fairy-tale voice told me that if you kept a wish secret long enough it would eventually come true. I bit my lip.

Akari the Estate Agent pulled up a chair. I forgot that we weren't talking and offered him a sip of Fanta. Akari had a plan. He said it was a plan that he had dreamed especially for us. His cinema venture had fallen through. No one wanted to go to the cinema in Sid Zouin, so he had decided to turn the garden behind his house, which was already a café, into a hotel. We, he had decided, were to be his very first guests.

'It is the most beautiful garden in the world,' he sighed, his eyes half closed. 'When the cinema seats have gone... Ha...' He clapped his hands. 'Then you will see.'

Mum said she thought it sounded lovely, but Bea still hadn't forgiven Akari for the murder of Snowy, and I was worried that if we went away from Marrakech Bilal wouldn't be able to find us when he came home. Akari extolled the virtues of Sid Zouin until he had moved himself to tears, and Mum pressed his hand and swore that it would be an honour for us to be the first guests at his hotel.

Mum promised Akari that as soon as our money arrived from England we were going to Sid Zouin. Every day she went to the bank to ask, but the man there just shook his turban at her and looked serious. We stopped eating at the cafés in the Djemaa El Fna and cooked in our room over the mijmar which smoked furiously under the broken bellows, making it impossible to breathe unless both doors were left open. The nights had become so cold Mum said sometimes she thought it was a good thing we were being forced to wait until spring before going to the country.

One morning early I was woken by her murmurings as she knelt on the mat. She sniffed between each prayer. In a pause that I hoped was the end I ventured, 'Mum...'

'Hello.'

I couldn't think what else to say. 'I can't sleep.'

'Neither can I,' she said, and she knelt over my bed and whispered, 'Would you like to go for a walk?'

We dressed quickly, careful not to wake Bea, and crept out into the beginnings of the morning. We walked hand in hand through the crisp, empty streets, the hoods of our burnouses warm and muffled round our ears. The maze of streets narrowed as we walked deep into the old walled city, the dawn lighting up the faded pink cement of the crumbling buildings.

We saw it from a distance, the wool street, in a flash of new white light. It lay in front of us, a carpet of dancing colours. The street was lined with factories where the wool was dyed and hung out to dry in skeins on lines between the buildings, and at night, when the wool was cut down, the snippets and loose ends of a multitude of colours fell to the ground. We arrived like thieves before the road sweepers and ran about scooping up handfuls of the soft new wool.

Mum stopped. She stood still with a wide smile on her face and let her handful of wool petals fall to the floor. 'I'll make dolls,' she said, 'with woollen hair.'

'For us?' I asked.

'No,' she yelled, 'dolls to sell. Now look for wool in black, yellow and red. Pieces long enough for hair.'

I searched the ground, draping each new strand over my arm until I had enough wool to make a hairpiece for even the most life-sized of dolls. Mum sorted the wool into separate skeins and tied them round her wrist. Then she knelt down and swept up a multicoloured pile of leftovers, motioning for me to turn around so she could pack them into my hood.

'Stuffing,' she explained.

Mum spent that whole day sewing the dolls. She made the bodies out of an old white T-shirt of Bea's and stuffed them tight with wool, poking it into the ends of their legs and arms with a pencil. She embroidered blue eyes and red mouths on to their smooth oval faces and sewed on hair in a middle parting. The first doll she finished had black hair that reached down to her waist.

'It looks like Mum,' Bea said.

She made a dress out of a pink-and-grey flowery skirt I hadn't worn since the Mellah. Mum had made it for me in Tunbridge Wells out of a cushion I didn't want to leave behind.

'You don't mind, do you?'

I shook my head.

She worked all day on her sewing-machine until there were three perfect dolls. Mary, Mary-Rose, and Rose-mary. Mum was delighted. 'Tomorrow we'll sell them in the market,' she laughed. 'And then all our troubles will be over.'

The next day we got up early and walked to the flea

market by the south gate of the Medina. We took a blanket which we spread on the ground, arranging our three dolls in the centre. The flea market was on the edge of a flat plain that stretched away to the mountains, the same mountains you could see from the flat roof of the Hotel Moulay Idriss, where it snowed all year round. From where I sat on the corner of the blanket it seemed that the plain was a desert of people, all selling mysterious objects from blankets of their own.

Mary, Mary-Rose and Rosemary attracted a great deal of attention, even at times drawing a crowd, but no one showed the slightest inclination to buy.

'It's not an exhibition,' Mum grumbled as the dolls were poked and admired but never bartered for.

As the afternoon began to fade away and the various salesmen and merchants packed up their blankets, we had no choice but to give up.

'I expect this is how Akari felt when no one wanted to go to the cinema,' Mum reflected.

I had never had a doll before and now I had three. They slept with me in my bed, becoming more and increasingly more demanding of my time. There were various complicated ministrations and attentions at particular and specific times of the day and night, and especially in the morning when Bea was at school and Mum was praying or on a visit to her bank.

CHAPTER TWENTY

Akari closed up his shop to take us to Sid Zouin. We arrived by communal taxi with three other men and a cage of rabbits. Akari's house was the first building in the village. It was a low, dark room full of tables and chairs. Men in white turbans sat in the gloom and drank coffee.

A silence fell as we entered and every man's eye fixed on Mum. 'This is Akari's café,' Akari said, and hurried us back out on to the street.

He opened a door in a high arch in the wall.

Akari had been right to sit in the Djemaa El Fna and cry for his garden. In Marrakech spring was just beginning, but in Akari's magic garden it was in full bloom. Almond trees drooped under snowdrifts of blossom. Petals from the peach and apricot trees covered the ground in a blanket of white: tiny oranges and lemons clustered among the leaves of trees that grew against the garden wall, barely visible behind a brier of pink roses that clung to its mud-baked bricks. In every remaining patch of grass, daisies, hollyhocks and snapdragons grew tall.

Our room was a short walk across the garden. It was built on to the back of the café, and if I stood by the adjoining wall I could hear the murmur of the men as they drank their coffee and talked. The room was white and newly painted and had two shelves built into the bricks. There was a mijmar in one corner and a pot to cook in. For sleeping there were straw mats and blankets. There was not a scorpion or even a cockroach in sight.

At the other end of the garden was a long, low room, built on top of the wall. It could only be reached by wooden steps and made me think of the witch's house in 'Hansel and Gretel'. It was called the Projection Room. Opposite the Projection Room was a whitewashed wall.

'That,' Akari said, 'is where the films are showing. The people sit on benches in the garden and watch the films in the wall.'

Now the whitewashed wall stood in the middle of the garden as if it knew it had no purpose, and all the benches were gone.

'Akari please start the cinema again,' Bea begged him, but he shook his head stubbornly. 'Now I am in the hotel business,' he declared.

I had only ever seen one film. It was a film of *Hamlet* in Russian with Arabic subtitles. Even Mum couldn't understand it. Mum said that Bea and I had sat through *Bambi* twice without a break at the Classic, but I didn't remember.

That night, as we were preparing for bed, two men burst into our room. They were dressed in the baggy trousers and loose shirts of men who worked in the fields, and they stared at Mum with bright, hopeful eyes. Mum stared blankly back at them. No one spoke. Then one of the men made a circle with his thumb and index finger and pointed through it with his other hand. Encouraged, the second man did the same, and I watched entranced as they stood in earnest mime. Bea put her hands over her face and began to giggle and Mum's bewildered frown knit into a furious flash of the eyes. She jumped up and in one swift movement shooed the men out like hens.

'What did they want?' I asked, but Mum couldn't stop

118

laughing long enough to tell me. Bea 'crossed her heart and hoped to die' she didn't know.

Early each morning a group of men, in trousers so full they could be skirts, arrived in the garden to make Akari's hotel dream come true. Where the benches for the outside cinema had been, a row of small rooms was to be built. The builders began by making bricks from mud and straw, casting them with oblong wedges in a wooden mould. Once the brick had set, it was tipped on to the ground to bake rock-hard in the sun. As the builders worked they chanted, filling the garden with a mysterious song that echoed between its walls. The chanting was led by the lead builder amidst a series of heavy breaths that matched the rhythm of his work. It was picked up and developed into a chorus by the others, eventually coming back to the first man who breathed new life into it and passed it on.

The whitewashed wall stayed where it was. Sometimes Bea and I would creep up into the Projection Room and stare at it for hours on end hoping to catch a story from the moving shadows thrown up by the men. When nothing happened I begged Bea to tell me the story of *Bambi*. Over and over again. There were bits of it she couldn't remember and she said it was the singing builders that were putting her off.

The men worked until midday, when they laid down their tools, ate their lunch and fell asleep under the almond trees. During their siesta Bea and I began to build our own house. I hoped it might be a summer house for Mary, Mary-Rose and Rosemary, but Bea had plans on a grander scale. She wanted it to be a home for us. We started, like the builders, by making bricks. We moulded our mud and straw by hand, kneading it into a cake with water. We carried our first brick to a secret place and watched over it jealously as it dried. When we had baked twelve bricks, Bea decided, building would begin.

On the day set for construction to start we were

disturbed by unusual movement in the Projection Room. Bea put her finger to her lips and gestured for me to follow. We crept through the garden, camouflaged by wild flowers, running from tree to tree for cover. When we reached the garden wall, Bea scrambled up the twisted wooden vine of a climbing rose and pulled me up after her. I stopped to rub my knee but Bea was already tip-toeing fast along the wall. We crouched under the Projection Room window and listened. The suppressed voices of a man and a woman arguing drifted out to us, drowned by the occasional twang of a guitar. Bea stretched up to look.

'There's a lady with white socks on,' she reported. 'One man with a beard, and another man with a beard and patches on his bottom.'

'Can I look?'

'All right. But be careful.'

I craned my neck and peered through the window. One of the men was trying to light the mijmar without using any candlewax or paper. Every time the woman tried to help he said in a very warning voice, 'Jeannie...'

The other man was tuning a guitar.

We ran along the wall, climbed down the rose vine and went to tell Mum. Mum brushed her hair and put on her purple caftan. She walked with us across the garden, up the wooden steps and knocked on the door of the Projection Room.

Jeannie started when she saw Mum, but the man who was called Scott gave up on the fire and came over and shook her hand. Mum told them we were living just across the garden, but that really we were from England. Jeannie and Scott said they had only just arrived from Canada when they had had the good luck to meet up with Akari.

'We had to get out of that city,' Scott explained. 'Poor Jeannie, she just couldn't stand to see another beggar.'

Jeannie shivered.

Pedro was from Argentina. He had dark curly hair that had been bleached in streaks by the sun. He sat on the windowsill and played his guitar softly.

'Pedro Patchbottom, Pedro Patchbottom,' we called through the open door of our room as Pedro and Mum sat deep in conversation over a pattern of cards that told your fortune. 'Please, Pedro Patchbottom, please come and build our house with us.'

'Later, later, I promise.' Pedro picked up a card on which a tall woman in a crown brandished a magic wand. 'This card you have chosen' – he looked deep into Mum's eyes without blinking – 'is a true card of power and . . .' – he paused – 'of love.'

The colour rose in Mum's face and she looked away.

'Mum . . .' I sidled into the room and sat close to her. 'When is Bilal coming back?'

Mum, who was about to reach for Pedro's magic card, let her hand fall into her lap. 'Bilal?'

'Bilal,' Bea reminded her from just inside the door.

And I repeated, 'When's he coming back?'

Pedro shuffled and reshuffled the cards.

Mum was lost for words. She looked blankly from me to Bea as if after all this time we should have forgotten who Bilal was. The rash that had been growing on the inside of my arm began to crawl with an army of ants. I scratched and scratched, my throat growing tighter, stinging my nose and squeezing the tears up into my eyes.

'I want to see Bilal,' I wailed, banging my fists on the floor. 'I want to see Bilal.' My chest ached and tears splashed into my mouth. Now I had started I couldn't stop. I could hear my voice, dull and desperate, calling hoarsely for Bilal, who I knew could never be found before I had to stop. Bea, swollen and blurred, watched me from the doorway. Her face was full of curiosity and a mild alarm. I searched between sobs for an excuse to stop, but each time Mum moved to comfort me I lashed out with my arms and held her off. I lay on the floor with my salty cheek against the tiles and howled with fury and exhaustion. Occasionally I scratched my arm which had turned a raw red.

'She'll be all right when she wakes up,' I heard Mum explain to Pedro before I fell into a black sleep.

Mum read aloud from the Ant and Bee book while I sat, wrapped in a blanket, on her lap.

'Feeling better?' she asked when it was finished, which was very soon as there was only one word on most of the pages.

'Are you going to write a letter to Bilal and tell him to come and visit?' I asked.

Mum flicked her finger through the book. 'I will,' she answered hesitantly, 'but first we'll have to wait until he writes to us. If I wrote a letter now I wouldn't know where to send it.'

There was a silence as Mum continued to flick through the pages. Bea lay on her back and stared up at the ceiling.

'Doesn't he know where we are then?' she asked.

'No,' Mum said.

'But if we don't know where Bilal is and Bilal doesn't know where we are,' I was working it out, 'then even if he wanted to write a letter he wouldn't be able to, would he? Would he?'

I was delighted by my theory.

Mum shifted me off her lap. 'He knew where to write when we were at the hotel for months and months...' She sneezed and then she began to cry. 'He knew where to write then.'

Bea came and held Mum's hand and stroked her hair. Mum went on crying. She kept blowing her nose between her fingers and flicking them clean outside into the grass like the Moroccans always did because they didn't believe in handkerchiefs. Mum said they thought the idea of carrying a piece of snot wrapped in material around in your pocket for days and days was disgusting. Bea kept talking to Mum. She was saying all sorts of things to try and cheer her up. I couldn't think of anything to say except, 'Oh Mum, please stop crying,' which made her cry even harder so that her shoulders shook.

Eventually Mum stood on the doorstep and blew her nose for the last time. Bea made supper from the bread and honey left over from breakfast and we sat in the garden and ate and watched the sun set on the other side of the stone wall.

'Let's stay here for as long as you want, Mum,' Bea said, and I agreed by nodding my head enthusiastically.

CHAPTER TWENTY-ONE

Akari's builders spent days digging ditches so that the walls of the hotel could begin underground. They sang and worked and pretended not to notice when we stole straw from their stack or borrowed the sieve to sift stones out of the dry earth. We decided against building foundations for our house even though Pedro tried his hardest to persuade us of their importance. 'One earthquake,' he said, 'and BANG!'

Every day we moulded new oblongs of mud and laid them in the sun to dry.

'Pedro Patchbottom, Pedro Patchbottom, please come and help us build our house.' Bea and I followed him through the garden, pulling at the patches of material that held his jeans in place, but he said if we wouldn't take his advice about the foundations then he couldn't help us any further. Pedro Patchbottom was lying. It was easy to see he just didn't want to help. All he ever wanted to do was to sit under the almond trees with Mum and listen to her read in her story-telling voice. She read to him from a thick book with a picture of a yogi on the front.

'What is a yogi?' I asked.

'A very holy man.'

'Like the Hadaoui?'

'Yes, a little like the Hadaoui.'

The picture on the front of the book was of an old man with long white hair sitting cross-legged with the soles of his feet turned upwards.

'What happened to him?' Bea asked.

'He's sitting in the lotus position,' Mum explained. 'It's called the lotus position because his feet look like the petals of a lotus flower.' She crossed her right foot over to demonstrate how it could be done and pulled the left into place, turning the soles of both feet upwards. She froze for five seconds before her legs sprang apart and she sighed with relief.

'Look, I can do it.' Bea sat straight-backed and proud, her legs bent in front of her like little flowers. She proved her point by remaining like that while Mum finished the chapter. As hard as I tried, I could only bend one leg at a time without tipping over backwards. For once I was grateful Bilal wasn't there.

'Is he holy like the man with the mantras?' I asked.

'That's right.' Mum was impressed. 'So you remember the guru?'

I did.

'And do you remember the mantra he gave you?'

Bea looked slyly at me.

'Don't tell anyone your secret word,' the Indian guru had said, 'but repeat this mantra every day one hundred times.' He tied a piece of dark red cotton around my wrist. I wanted to tell him I could only count to four which was how old I was, but the room was dark and thick with incense and Mum had told me to try hard and behave.

There were a lot of people waiting to be given mantras. The Indian guru, John had said, was only in London for a few days and we were lucky to catch him before we set off for Morocco in the van. Out of all the people who had come to see the guru I was the first to be taken into his room because I was the youngest. As I waited for Bea, and then Mum, to come back out, I could feel people staring at me. I played with my new bracelet and said my mantra over and over, wondering what would happen if I were ever to reach a hundred.

As soon as Bea had seen the guru she came and stood very close to me and whispered menacingly in my ear, 'I'll tell mine if you tell yours.'

I flushed and my heart began to beat with the effort of pretending to be deaf. I kept my eyes fixed on a woman who wore a dress covered in tiny round mirrors. She had a duffle coat over the top.

Eventually Bea gave up.

At some point on a long journey by van or train or communal taxi, I regretted my pious attitude and relented. But Bea had changed her mind. 'You had your chance,' she said, 'and you missed it.'

I pleaded and begged, even offering to tell mine first, but she was hard as steel, open to no bribes and holier than thou.

It was late in the afternoon and Mum still lay with Pedro under the almond trees. Bea and I sat on the garden wall and waited for the singing women to return from the fields. They travelled to and from their work in open trucks, their bright caftans fluttering over the heads of the babies that slept on their backs. We listened for their singing when the trucks were just a cloud on the road, and as they drew near we perched on the very edge of the wall and prepared to wave. The trucks rattled down the one street into the village in a burst of noise and colour. The women wore scarves over their hair and the shiny cloth of their dresses stood out in blocks of pink and green. They didn't wave back. Their rich voices filled the afternoon quiet, soon fading away again as the trucks, half empty now, rumbled out along the road.

'All right then...' Bea said when the dust in the street had resettled. I knew what she was about to suggest. I could tell she had been thinking about the mantra. 'I'll tell mine if you tell yours.'

'All right,' I began, but just as I was forming the words in my mouth into my unspoken prayer, I realized I'd forgotten it.

'Go on then,' Bea was impatient.

I caught my confession just in time. I turned to her with great solemnity. 'Don't tell anyone your secret word,' I said in the guru's husky voice.

Bea nearly pushed me off the wall. 'Helufa!' she cursed as she clambered down the rose vine.

'I'll tell you tomorrow. I promise,' I called, my moment of triumph fading fast.

'You had your chance and you missed it.' Bea danced across the garden and slammed the door into our room.

I sat on the wall and wondered how it was that Bea always won, whatever the game. However hard I copied and stored the rules, at the last moment she always twisted them, added something new, and won. I tried to conjure up the missing word. I had a suspicion it had been forgotten a very long time ago, long before I had begun offering to swop it in the back of the van. I concentrated hard and hoped my mantra would separate itself from all the other words I knew. I waited, watching the sun set slowly over the fields as the crickets whistled and every cock in the village crowed the end of the day.

CHAPTER TWENTY-TWO

I woke up to find I was lying in thick grass. It was the middle of the night and the air was full of the sounds of animals. Donkeys screaming to one another, dogs barking, chickens squawking and the songs of birds that never sang at night. All around my head a thousand crickets hummed and buzzed. I shifted in my blanket. I was so tightly wrapped I could hardly move my arms. Bea was lying next to me, similarly wrapped, softly and peacefully sleeping.

I struggled to sit up. I could see the open doorway of our house flickering in candlelight, but not a shadow to be seen of Mum. Then I heard voices from across the garden. Jeannie worrying and crying and Pedro swearing in his own language. The voices moved nearer, and my mother appeared with Scott, half dragging, half carrying, a limping Pedro. Jeannie zigzagged through the trees. She had nothing on except a pair of Aertex knickers.

'My God, I can't believe this is happening,' she wailed. Her body was white and lumpy in the moonlight.

Scott was wearing blue pyjamas a little like my own, except I never wore mine for sleeping. Mum was still dressed in her caftan. Pedro limped naked between them. They laid him gently in the grass. He moaned and closed his eyes.

'You silly fool,' Mum laughed fondly and kissed him on

128

the lips. Pedro moaned even louder and then began to laugh.

Bea woke up. 'What's happened?' she asked, untangling herself from the blanket.

'Pedro jumped out of the Projection Room window,' Mum said as if it were an everyday occurrence.

'Why?'

Pedro opened his eyes. 'Because where I come from that's what we do.'

Scott was feeling Pedro's leg between the ankle and the knee. 'I don't think it's broken.'

Pedro groaned.

'You've probably just sprained it.'

'Do you think it's safe to go inside yet?' Jeannie asked. She was shivering. Mum offered her my blanket.

'No, never go back inside.' Pedro was adamant. He shifted on to his elbow. 'Not until the animals are quiet.'

We sat in the grass and listened to the alarm of every bird and animal for miles and miles around.

'I was sitting up reading, and feeling unusually peaceful and happy,' Mum said, 'when I heard a convoy of articulated lorries travelling at great speed down the village road. I carried on reading and then I thought: how can there be a convoy of lorries travelling at great speed through Sid Zouin? It wasn't until the house began to shake that I realized it was an earthquake. An earthquake! I thought. How lovely.'

Pedro sat up and looked at her as if she were mad.

'And then I remembered that I was meant to be a responsible adult. I grabbed the children and carried them out into the garden, like you're supposed to, but the most fantastic thing was' – she looked at us, her eyes soft with pride – 'they both slept through the whole thing.'

Bea was furious. 'You should have woken me,' she said.

I lay back and pressed my body through the dewy grass, hard against the earth. I was hoping to catch a last tremor.

129

'I'm a very heavy sleeper,' I could tell Bilal or Aunty Rose or anyone. 'I even sleep through earthquakes.'

We stayed up all night waiting for the animals to quiet and listening to Pedro's earthquake stories. When he told how at the first rumble he had jumped out of bed, flung himself through the nearest window only to sprain his ankle and hit his head on a brick, no one could restrain themselves from laughing.

With the glimmer of morning we discovered the café to be unshaken and the Projection Room, much to Pedro's annoyance, was still safely perched on the wall. The only thing in the garden that had suffered any damage was Bea's and my nearly finished house. It lay transformed into a pile of broken bricks.

Pedro cheered up immediately. 'Foundations ...' he said. 'What did I tell you? One earthquake and ...'

'We know,' Bea said, 'and BANG!'

The Cadi who was the mayor of the village examined Pedro's ankle and declared it sprained.

'But badly sprained,' Pedro insisted.

From then on the seven wooden steps that led up to the Projection Room became an impossible hurdle. Mum invited Pedro to move in with us. Bea was not pleased. Bea was so angry I couldn't decide if I minded one way or the other. All the same I joined her in a 'persecute Pedro Patchbottom' campaign that ended a week later when we rose at dawn to unpick his one and only pair of trousers. We worked away through the early morning until his trousers hung unpatched and feebly together in a web of white cotton. Pedro was still sleeping naked under his blanket when Mum sprang up and slapped us both, fast and sharp with the flat of her hand. Then she got back into bed and slept until it was nearly time for lunch.

By the time the Sufis arrived Pedro had forgiven us and

his trousers were repatched and wearable again. The Sufis were two Americans on a pilgrimage to Algeria. They were on their way to visit the Zaouia, a mosque where the third Sufi sheikh, Sheikh Bentounes, lived.

As Akari's hotel rooms were still unfinished, the American men were to sleep in the garden. Mum sat up with them. She had a thousand questions to ask. She wanted to learn the ritual breathing techniques they used in prayer. The two Americans agreed that it wasn't something you could learn in a night and that if she was really interested she should go to the Zaouia and learn all these things for herself.

Mum's eyes sparkled.

Pedro played sad songs on his guitar. His songs grew sadder and louder as the night wore on. Then they switched into his own language and took over the conversation.

I forced myself to stay awake, keeping a watchful eye on Mum, convinced that if I let my guard drop for even a moment, she would slip out of the garden and turn into a Sufi.

The Black Hand was a disembodied hand that travelled the world strangling its victims. The Black Hand left one clue on the necks of its victims. The sooty print of its thumb. I heard its tread on the stairs.

One. Thump. Silence.

Two. Thud. Still. Waiting stillness. Strangling quiet.

Three . . .

And then the rattle of the doorknob as it . . . as its fingers twisted . . . as the handle turned . . .

I woke up bathed in sweat.

The Sufis were gone and Mum was nowhere to be seen.

'Mummeeeee!' I wailed into the dark, my heart breaking. I sat on the doorstep and howled. 'Mummeeeee!'

An irritable and sleepy voice grumbled from inside the

131

room. 'Oh please shut up, darling, and get back into bed.'
It was Mum.

Mum began to pray again, facing east on her mat. She
practised yoga positions, including the lotus, and talked
about a new adventure. The more restless she became the
more Pedro enthused about spending the whole summer
at Sid Zouin. Bea, having worked through to the last
lesson in her book, said she should really be getting back
to school, preferably in England. I thought about Bilal
searching for us, wandering through the cafés, standing
in the empty rooms of the Hotel Moulay Idriss. I practised
tightrope walking on the garden wall, threw myself into
handstands that were meant to turn into backflips but
never did, and tried to pluck up the courage to extinguish
the burning head of a match in my open mouth.

Bea and I sat in the taxi and waited for Mum and Pedro
to say goodbye. They stood together in the arched
doorway of the garden wall and held hands.
    'Come on,' we whined at intervals.
    Scott and Jeannie didn't come to see us off. Jeannie
hadn't forgiven Mum for refusing to listen to her offers of
advice. 'That language will get them into trouble,' she
had warned and, 'Children need discipline.'
    'I had plenty of discipline,' Mum said, 'and it didn't do
me any good.'
    Pedro stood in the street and watched our car as it drove
away. His face looked sad. Mum put her hand out of the
side window and waved but she didn't turn round.
    As soon as Pedro was out of sight, she began to explain
her plan: 'We'll stay in Marrakech for a few nights, wait
for some money to arrive and then we're off to Algiers to
visit the Zaouia.'
    'What about school?' Bea said.
    'And what about Bilal?'

'If Bilal's in Marrakech,' Mum assured me, 'we'll be sure to find him.'

'The Gnaoua might know, or the Fool,' I suggested, 'or the Nappy Ladies at the hotel.'

Moulay Idriss welcomed us with smiles of surprise, and tea, and explained there was not one spare room in the hotel. Not even for a night. The Nappy Ladies appeared in the doorway. They had seen us from the terrace of the second floor. Moulay Idriss invited them to join us in his abundantly cushioned room and drink a second glass of tea. Mum blushed. The crushed pink velvet of her favourite trousers were stretched tight to bursting over the legs of one of the ladies. Mum had made these trousers on her sewing-machine and worn them every day for a week, until one morning, after queuing with me for the toilet on the landing for over half an hour, she came back to our room to find them gone. Mum stared at the pink legs crossed in front of her and up at the open smiling face of the nappy thief.

'Of course I always knew it was her,' she said afterwards, 'but to taunt me! She must have run and put them on when she saw us arrive.'

Once three polite glasses of tea had been drunk and Mum had given up on Moulay Idriss to find us a room, we set off for the Djemaa El Fna to look for Bilal. Mum refused the Ladies' offer to mind our bags.

We wandered from café to café searching out a familiar face. The square, lit with its bulbs of light and smelling warm of city food, lulled me with memories and made me happy to be home. We set down our bags at the large open café where we had first met Luigi Mancini. Mum ordered meat tajine and went to buy cigarettes from the man who sold them singly in the square. The Fool appeared at our table. He smiled, his one tooth hovering in his mouth as if it were about to drop.

'It's the Fool! It's the Fool!' I sang with delight. I held on to his hand until he sat down.

Bea and I cross-examined him. 'Bilal? Khadija? Aunty Rose? The Hadaoui? Bilal? Bilal? Bilal? . . .'

The Fool nodded and smiled and repeated each name lovingly. I searched his eyes for information. They were dark and far away. 'Bilal . . .' he mused.

Mum returned to our table with Luna and Umbark. Luna lifted her veil and kissed Bea and me on both cheeks. She gazed into our faces. 'From day to day they change,' she said, tears glistening in the edges of her eyes. Luna sat down. It wasn't us but Luna who had changed. She had swollen up strangely since we went away and the blue veins in her face, flowing so near the surface, gave her a glassy look. Luna noticed the red rash in the crook of my arm. I had rolled up the sleeve of my caftan to cool it after an attack of itching. Luna inspected the raw and slimy rash. It ached under her scrutiny.

Mum dug into her bag and brought out the round tin she had bought from the salesman in Sid Zouin. After my arm had been shown to the Cadi, Pedro, Scott, Jeannie, and almost every other inhabitant of the village, a travelling salesman had inspected it and assured us he possessed the cure. The one and only cure. He sold us a small, flat tin of cream. It wasn't until he had trotted out of town on his donkey that Mum realized the tin didn't actually open. Pedro nearly broke a finger in his attempt to wrench it apart and Scott tried each one of the sharp instruments on his penknife. Like my arm the tin was inspected first by the Cadi and then by every other member of the village before it was finally returned to us, battered, but still firmly closed.

Mum passed the tin around the table. When it reached the Fool, he held it up to the light and nodded thoughtfully over its secret contents. Without a word he pocketed it in the folds of his djellaba.

I soaked my bread in the steaming juice of the mutton tajine, burning my fingers as I ate. Luna and Umbark had neither seen nor heard of Bilal since he left with the Hadaoui.

'Maybe they are travelling in the desert. He and the Hadaoui,' Luna said, and Mum agreed and told them about her plan to make a pilgrimage to the Zaouia.

We stayed that night with Luna and Umbark in their tiny room, and the next day Mum went alone to visit her bank.

Luna was taking Bea and me to lunch. 'I want you to meet some friends of mine,' she said.

Luna's friends were an English family who lived in the new French city. They had two children. A baby younger than Mob and a boy called Jake who clung to his mother's legs as she moved about the kitchen.

Bea was very impressed with lunch. So was I. Mostly it was mashed potato. We had three helpings each. I ate my meal in greedy silence while Bea talked. She told Jake's mother Sophie all about school. What she had learnt there and what she hadn't and how many times the children got beaten, and about the time the stick broke. She told her things that she usually kept to herself.

After lunch I played with Jake on a red plastic telephone. He rang up Father Christmas and I rang Luigi Mancini. Bea helped Sophie with the washing-up.

I could hear Bea telling Sophie all about how Mum was going to go and live in a mosque with lots of sheikhs who sat all day in the lotus position and that really she didn't want to go. Luna interrupted her to say that Mum was only going to visit for a short time, not to live, but Bea said she didn't care – she still didn't want to go.

As we were about to leave, Bea turned to Sophie. 'Could I stay with you when Mum goes to the mosque?' she asked, her eyes round with hope.

Sophie was silent. 'If that's all right with your Mummy,'

she said finally, hesitantly, 'then of course that would be fine with us.' She glanced towards a closed door through which the clattering of her husband's typewriter could be heard, muffled between long silences. 'Yes I'm sure that would be fine,' she said again as she opened the front door.

We met up with Mum in the Djemaa El Fna. Her money hadn't arrived and she was in a bad mood. I waited anxiously for Bea to break the news. Whenever I caught her eye, she looked away. Luna said nothing.

'We'll stay one more night with you if that's all right.' Mum looked to Luna. 'And then we'll be off. I think if we get a couple of good lifts it should only take a day to get there.'

'You're going to hitch?'

'Yes. I'll get the bank to wire the money through to Algiers when it arrives.'

There was a pause in the conversation. This was Bea's chance. I kicked her under the table. She kicked me back hard and kept quiet.

Then the Fool appeared with our tin. He held it under my nose and with a flourish twisted off the top. Inside was a round of hard black wax, a little like a crayon.

'This shoe polish,' the Fool spoke slowly, and Luna translated his halting words, 'is not so good. This shoe polish is in fact very, very old.'

While Mum sorted through our things, deciding what to take and what to leave behind, Bea said in the most casual of her voices, 'Oh, Mum, would it be all right if I didn't come?'

Mum wavered momentarily and continued to pack.

'I asked Sophie if I could stay with her and she said yes. She said as long as it's all right with you. She said ...'

Mum withdrew a T-shirt of Bea's and put it to one side.

'Fine,' she said flatly, 'if that's what you want.'

Bea opened her mouth to continue the argument and then closed it again.

Mum didn't speak.

'Goodnight,' she said eventually when she had finished packing. There was one large bag for me and Mum, and a smaller one for Bea.

'Goodnight,' we both said in uncomfortably cheerful voices and she left the room to join Luna and Umbark on their terrace.

Bea stood at the top of the tiled steps of Sophie's house and watched us go. Sophie stood behind her in a dressing-gown and waved.

'We'll be back soon,' I called before we turned a corner and lost sight of her.

'I never thought she'd say yes,' Bea had whispered to me the night before once Mum was safely on the terrace. But we both agreed there was no going back.

CHAPTER TWENTY-THREE

Mum and I stood at the edge of the road and stretched out our thumbs. Most of the cars that passed were lorries and mostly they were going the wrong way. They crowded up to the gates of the city with full loads of water melons, oranges, chickens and sheep. I thought of all the chickens that had been eaten on the last day of Ramadan. Every family in the hotel had bought one, cluttering the terrace with wilting, shackled birds that squawked in terror on the morning of their last day. They hung, waiting to be cooked, their necks broken and their feet tied. I thought of Snowy and her beady eyes and the way she liked to peck corn from the cracks between the fingers of your hand.

'In the end they'll have to turn round and come back,' Mum said as we watched the stream of traffic heading into the city. The sky had turned a pale green with the rising mist, but it was still cold.

A tall blond man strolled out of the city gates and began to walk towards us. He stopped a little way in front and took up a waiting position, his eyes fixed on the road.

'Where are you going?' Mum called to him eventually, when two cars had failed to stop for either him or us. He was very thin and his trousers looked like he had made them himself. 'Where are you going?' Mum asked again, when he came near.

The Hitcher raised his hands in a questioning gesture and muttered something, his voice full of muddy words.

Mum repeated her question in French and then in Arabic. If Bea were here, I thought, she'd make him understand. Mum pointed down the road. 'Algiers?'

'Ah, Algiers.' He nodded and smiled. 'Algiers.'

Not long after, a truck stopped. Mum and I sat in the high cab with the driver. The Hitcher climbed into the open back and settled himself among the straw and droppings of a recent load of sheep.

'Algiers?' Mum asked as we climbed in.

'Algiers?' she asked again more anxiously as we began to pick up speed. The driver raised one eyebrow and pressed his foot hard on the accelerator.

Our truck rattled along in a breathtaking race. Everything on the road had to be overtaken. Even a single donkey warranted an ear-piercing blast of the horn to signal our approach. I kept my eyes glued to the road. I was sure if I removed them for a second we would dissolve in a splintering crash of metal.

The sun rose slowly in the sky, heating the truck into a burning grid as I watched the road unfold. With a great effort and tearing of eyes I forced myself to twist away. I peered at the Hitcher. He lay face down in a pile of straw with his shirt over his head.

The driver brought the truck to an abrupt stop. He slid out of his seat and, taking a carefully wrapped parcel of food, walked over to a nearby tree. Mum and I climbed stiffly after him. The driver looked unencouraging as we approached but the tree was the only shade in sight and the sun was beating a hole through the top of my head. Little sparks of white light danced before my eyes.

'Mad dogs and Englishmen,' Mum sang half-heartedly.

Mum and I shared an orange and ate half the loaf of bread she had in her bag. The driver finished his lunch and fell asleep sitting upright against the trunk of the tree.

'Are we nearly there?' I asked, and Mum said she wasn't sure but she thought about halfway.

The Hitcher slept through the afternoon and only woke up when we stopped at a house that served supper. 'Algiers?' he asked as if he had just remembered who he was.

The driver shook his head and Mum said, 'No, but I think we should be there soon. We must have been going for twelve hours at least.'

'Henning.' The Hitcher pointed to himself.

After we'd eaten and sat for a while listening to the unintelligible crackle of the radio, the driver made his way back to the truck. It was night and the air was warm and thick with the smell of earth.

'Can we sit in the back with Henning?' I asked, dreading the surly racket of the cab.

Henning began to chat happily to Mum.

'It was only recently,' Mum interrupted him as if she understood every one of his words and was simply carrying on the conversation, 'that I became really interested in the Sufi.'

Henning said something of which only the words 'Henning' and 'Algiers' were recognizable.

I lay back and looked up at the sky. The stars here were different from the stars in Marrakech. They were jagged and white and they crowded out the sky. Under the low murmur of Henning's monologue I listened to the crickets and the stillness of the air.

'We're not moving,' Mum said all of a sudden, interrupting everything. 'I've only just realized, we're not actually going anywhere.' She stood up and looked through the narrow window into the cab. 'He's asleep,' she said. 'He's sitting there and he's fast asleep.' Then she began to laugh. 'Well, it doesn't look like we'll be arriving tonight after all.' Mum lay down in the straw. 'Tomorrow. God willing. Inshallah.' And she closed her eyes.

Henning was wide awake. He sat directly across from

me and talked, fixing me with eyes that glowed pale. Sunstroke, Mum would have said if she'd been awake. Henning talked on, hardly pausing for breath. I set my mind on the distant crackle of the radio and the chorus of crickets that hummed all around the truck. A dog began to whine, bursting into a frenzied bark. Henning hardly blinked. His words were heavy and laden and from time to time he stretched his throat and gulped.

I kept to my side of the truck. 'Sufi, Medina, Coca-Cola, Coca-Cola,' I sang quietly. 'Ramadan, Calisha, earrings and jellybeans.' My voice gained strength. 'Waa waa Khadija.'

Henning was silent.

'Waa waa Khadija,' I quavered. 'Waa waa believe her. Waa waa cat fever. Waa waa Bea, Bilal. Beetroot, Beetrootlal. Lal lal Beeeelal.' My voice rose and fell in an ever more practised imitation of Om Kalsoum.

Henning had stopped talking. I carried on mumbling and singing small victorious phrases. 'The grand old Duke of York, Sheikh Bentounes, hey Helufa, he had ten thousand men ... Mashed potato ...'

Henning began to snore.

The air was sharp and cold and there was a pink sunrise turning the sky white. Our truck groaned up a steep hill. I stared at the wall of rock stretching away from the road in a gentle curve. I watched as it dissolved into sky. On the other side, the road fell away in a gulf of nothing. Sunrise and the occasional wheeling bird. The tyres scrunched along the cliff, sending showers of dry earth and pebbles falling forever over the edge. We were climbing a mountain. The road was not a road but a narrow ledge. A flat plain unfolded below, stretching away like a sea of brown paper. Scorched fields dotted with struggling trees and specks that might be goats nibbling a rare new overnight shoot.

Through the window of the high cab I could see the head and shoulders of the driver. He had one hand on the wheel as he steered the truck. He looked as though he might be whistling. I woke Mum. 'We're in the mountains.'

She stood up shakily. First she looked at the rock-face on her side of the truck and then she peered over my side into the chasm below. She started back.

'I don't remember there being mountains on the map,' she said. 'But then again ...'

She gazed in silence at the stretch of plain, at the fields and tiny houses and at the changing colour of the earth.

'Mum,' I tried to coax her back.

'Yes?' She continued to hang, her arms and head dangling over the edge.

'Mum, please ... ' I begged, pulling at her dress.

'I hope nothing decides to come the other way.' She squinted past the driver to the steep and narrow road that twisted in a single lane ahead.

As the morning wore on the truck slowed to a crawl. Black and white goats looked down at us from paths in the rock. It was cooler in the mountains and the air was sweet and fresh. Mum draped a cloth over Henning's head. 'So he won't be so crazy when he wakes up,' she said.

Mum and I finished our loaf of bread and ate an orange each. The juice stuck to my hands and face and my arm began to itch.

'I need to go to the toilet.'

Mum banged on the window of the cab. The driver looked round, taking his eyes off the road for a long, terrifying minute. I scratched my arm ferociously.

'Stop. Stop. Arrête,' Mum mouthed at him through the glass. The driver creased his eyes in incomprehension and turned away.

'I need to go to the toilet,' I moaned.

Mum slapped my hand to stop me scratching. 'I'll hold on to you and you pee over the edge,' she said, hoisting me up on to the metal wall.

Henning lay motionless under his scarf.

Mum held me tight by the arms while I squatted on the ledge and tried to pee on to the road and not into the truck. As I was lifted back to safety a horn began to blare. It wasn't our horn. It came from further up the mountain. It wound round the corners nearer and louder with each bend of the road. Our truck slowed right down and stopped. The driver opened his door and got out.

'Algiers?' Henning asked. He had woken up.

A truck almost identical to ours but carrying a half-load of sheep came to a halt a few feet away. The two men stood in the middle of the road and argued. They were making a plan. Eventually they both turned round and got back into their trucks. First the other man backed off a little. Then we began to move forward, inch by inch straight towards the cliff edge.

Henning buried his head in his hands. Mum and I scrambled over to the safer side.

The other truck nuzzled into the rock-face, its wheels spinning as they tilted up the wall. We edged forward until the two cabs were side by side, their walls scraping and grating above the engine and the braying of the frightened sheep. Our truck lurched. A shower of loose earth and stones fell away from the ledge and cascaded down the sheer cliff. I listened with burning ears for the slide of our wheels slipping off the road. Mum pulled me to the back of the truck. I held on to her and prepared to jump. Henning kept his face buried.

We progressed scrape by scrape with slow grinds. I had forgotten how to breathe. I gasped, my mouth open, sucking and swallowing the air into my chest. My chest ached. There was a point right between my ribs that was as raw as my arm. I wanted to lie down and go to sleep.

A fat, white sheep watched me with concern. I held its liquid eye as it moved slowly past until with a loud blast of the horn our truck pulled free and screeched into the middle of the road.

Henning leapt up and began to dance. The skin on my face had frozen with the wait and now it began to tingle.

'Are we nearly there?' I asked, but I didn't expect anyone to know.

'Don't stare,' Mum said, as we watched the driver unpack his lunch.

We had stopped on top of the mountain. There were crystals of purple glass scattered over the ground. Amethyst, Mum said they were. The amethyst, which was a jewel, grew in rocks like a hard and shiny animal. I wanted to collect it. All of it, or just some of it and take it away, but the rocks were too heavy to lift. In Marrakech I had seen women selling earrings and bracelets made of amethyst. If I could just carry some away, Bea and I could sell it on a stall while Bilal told jokes and did backflips to attract a crowd. We'd make our fortunes and live in a magic palace like Luigi Mancini's that floated from place to place so that when Mum wanted an adventure we wouldn't have to hitch.

Henning sat on a rock and watched the driver eating his food. He pretended that he wasn't watching, but I could see he was following the driver's every mouthful.

I tried to make him help me. I wanted him to crack apart one of the stones so that it would be small enough to carry. I wanted him to lift one up and crash it down so that it would splinter into tiny pieces. Pieces the right size to sell on a stall. He refused to understand and continued to watch the driver's every move.

Mum sat with a straight back and meditated.

In the late afternoon we drove into a vineyard. We had

all moved into the front of the truck to get out of the sun, and as we passed through a faded wooden gate the driver turned and gave us his first smile. He stopped the truck in front of a row of stone buildings and turned off the engine. A dog ran out of a shed and jumped up at him. He kicked the dog affectionately and stretched.

The driver wasn't going any further. We had arrived at his vineyard and that was as far as he went. But before we continued our journey he insisted we accompany him on a guided tour. We wandered listlessly down rows of green vines, their leaves scattered with grapes too small to eat. The driver glowed with pride. He kept up a running commentary as we walked, kicking his dog from time to time with an indulgent smile.

'Algiers?' Mum asked when the tour was over. The driver pointed us along the rough track that led away from his farm and we said thank you and goodbye.

Mum, Henning and I stood on the dirt track with our eyes fixed hopefully on the horizon. Nothing appeared.

We began to walk.

'I can't help thinking,' Mum said after some time, 'that this might be one of those roads that nothing ever comes down.'

It began to grow dark. Once it started to grow dark you only had to notice and it was dark. It seemed pointless to keep on walking. We sat down on a wall.

I closed my eyes and imagined Bea lying in a bedroom full of toys under a smooth white sheet, too full of mashed potato to sleep. Maybe she'd go back to visit Aunty Rose and Aunty Rose would give her presents and home-made biscuits and glasses of lemonade. She would have Khadija all to herself and then if Bilal came back she might tell him that me and Mum had left her behind and he'd feel sorry for her and she'd become his favourite. I wondered what Mum's face would have looked like if I'd said that

I wasn't going to the Zaouia either. Little shivers ran
across my skin. I knew I could never have done it.

I must have fallen asleep because when Ali stepped out of
the darkness and introduced himself I woke up with a
start. Ali knew of somewhere we could spend the night. It
was a mud hut with a roof made of straw. The hut had
one room and it was round. Moonlight flooded in through
the doorway and lit up the rush mats that covered the
floor.

Henning had a pack of cards. Henning, Mum and I sat
in a circle and played snap. Ali had disappeared without
a word as soon as we were settled in. It was very hard to
play snap by moonlight but it was the only game we could
get Henning to understand. Every time someone said
'snap' Mum lit a match to see if they were right. The
game went on for ever, and when eventually Henning
won we started again. I was too hungry to sleep.

We heard them before they arrived. A murmur of voices
and the occasional giggle as they drew near. We stopped
playing and listened. Ali appeared in the doorway. He
was carrying something in his arms. He squatted down
over our cards and unwrapped his bundle. Three round
white loaves of bread. Their hot, sweet smell filled the hut.
Ali urged us to eat.

'You must thank your sister from us.' Mum was deeply
moved. 'Many times.'

There were two other boys with Ali. They hovered in
the doorway. One of them carried a portable record-
player and the other gripped a pile of records. While we
devoured Ali's bread, his friends set up the machine and
soon the heavy, sweeping sounds of Egyptian music wove
magic into the air like scent.

We found where the track joined the main road and

waited in hope for our next lift. Ali and his friends had packed up their records and disappeared at dawn. They had to milk the goats, they said. After they were gone Mum mumbled something about making an early start. Then she fell asleep. Now it was scorchingly hot. I tucked my hair into a turban. When I wore it I could decide whether I wanted to be a boy or a girl.

A car stopped. It was the first car we had seen since leaving the vineyard. It was driven by a French lady who was on her way to look at rock paintings in the Sahara Desert. She invited us to go with her. I was very keen. One of my new ambitions was to see a mirage and according to Tintin books the desert was the place to find one. Mum, I could see, was tempted, but she had set her heart on the Zaouia and she would not be persuaded otherwise. The French lady was going to spend the night at the house of another French lady on her way to the Sahara and she said the least we could do was to accept one night's hospitality. The next morning she would drop us at the Zaouia herself.

CHAPTER TWENTY-FOUR

Henning, Mum and I stood in the courtyard of the mosque and waited for someone to appear. Henning had been told several times that this was the Zaouia and not Algiers and that Algiers was further down the road, but he followed us into the courtyard anyway.

A man came out to meet us. He had a wild red beard that submerged his face up to the eyes, and his mouth was a crescent when he smiled. We followed him into a room made completely of tiles like the Hammam where we washed in Marrakech. We sat on cushions and drank mint tea while Mum talked. The man listened and kept up his smile, sometimes interrupting her with a mumbled and ecstatic 'Allah akhbar', which I knew meant 'God is great', and he made me think of the Hadaoui and wonder if they knew each other.

I waited for hours and hours for Mum to finish talking. Henning had fallen asleep on his cushion and every so often he began to snore. I shook his shoulder so that he groaned and rolled over and there was a gap of a few minutes before he started up again.

After a final pot of tea the red-bearded man led us out into the courtyard. He walked us through the garden to the gates, which he opened himself. For a moment Mum looked blankly at him.

'We can't stay?' She asked, incredulous, her voice rising to a shout. 'But we've come so far!'

I pulled at her dress. Don't shout. Don't shout, I prayed. Mum's voice rang through the calm courtyard with its rose bushes and its well-raked garden. The holy man walked calmly away without a backward glance and disappeared into the mosque. We stood in the road: Mum flushed with anger, me with my eyes on the ground, and Henning, sleepy and baffled, a little cheerful smile on his lips that now we would be travelling together after all on the last lap of the journey.

We went straight to the British consulate in Algiers to see if our money had arrived. It hadn't.

'But that's impossible,' Mum insisted.

'I'm afraid it's very possible,' the clerk said and grinned as if he had told a funny joke. Mum sat down on a bench and burst into tears. The British consulate clerk turned pale. He pulled out a large newly ironed handkerchief and edged round the counter to comfort her.

'I absolutely don't have a penny,' she sobbed, 'and then there's the child ...'

He looked over at me. I was standing by a potted plant pretending to be someone else. I'd prefer to starve! I thought grandly as I watched him produce a thick leather wallet from his trouser pocket and offer personally, in a hushed voice, to lend my mother money. We sat on the steps of the British consulate while Mum wiped her eyes and counted out the notes.

'What with your father and the Moroccan postal service it's a miracle anything ever gets through at all,' she sighed.

A man who was originally from Hastings invited us to stay. He had come to the consulate to apply for a permit to marry his girlfriend. He was teaching English as a foreign language and his girlfriend who was German was teaching German.

'What about Henning?' I asked. He had gone off to find a friend of a friend. We hadn't said goodbye or anything.

'Oh, Henning will be all right,' Mum said, and we followed the teacher along a wide avenue of orange trees.

We stayed in the teacher's flat for a few days and then in the flat of a friend of his who also taught languages. Mum made me sing to them and asked them to guess what language it was. They pretended they didn't know. I told them it was the language I had used in my last life. No one said anything but I could tell they were impressed.

Every day we returned hopefully to the consulate to ask about our money. Every day the answer was the same. Rather than outstay our welcome with the teachers, Mum decided we would wait for our money in a Youth Hostel she had heard was cheap and on the outskirts of Algiers. We had a little borrowed money left and we took a bus.

The bus ride, it turned out, was a full day's journey and we arrived at the Youth Hostel late in the afternoon. The Youth Hostel was a large white house covered in a clinging pink vine of bougainvillaea. It stood in the shade of a palm tree and the land behind it ran down to the sea. I was glad we had come.

'Of course. A room for two.' The man who appeared seemed pleased to see us. 'A room that looks over the sea with two beds.' Then he frowned a deep frown and reconsidered. 'But first there is a question you must answer.' He fixed Mum with an interrogative stare. 'Are you, or have you ever been, a member of the Youth Hostels Association?'

Mum was tired. She reached for my hand. 'Is that important?'

'Important? But of course it is important. Otherwise there is no point in a Youth Hostel. I have to abide by the rules of the Association.' He pointed to a small triangular plaque by the side of the door. His word 'Association' lasted for a long time.

Mum clutched my hand so tightly her rings cut into my flesh. 'I am a foreigner in your country and the book of Islam tells me that it is the duty of every servant of Allah to give hospitality to strangers. Surely,' she said, her voice calm, 'it is more important to abide by the laws of Islam than by those of a Youth Hostel.'

There was a silence and then his face changed. 'You are right, of course ...' he said and he showed us to our room.

There was no one else staying at the Youth Hostel. The owner's nephew worked there as a caretaker and slept in a small room by the kitchen. Each morning before setting off for school he left a plate of bread and dates on the table for our breakfast. His uncle was a sculptor. He lived in a house in the village where he would often hold parties and the people who came to them were also sculptors or painters or what Mum called the Intellectual Set. Some were from the village and some travelled a long way especially. Sometimes the only food at the party was a tray of biscuits that I was never offered. One night I helped myself. The biscuit crumbled in my mouth and tasted of majoun. I ate another, and then the tray was lifted up above my head and whisked away and a lady in a shimmering red caftan tousled my hair and laughed into my face. I spent the evening looking for Bea. I wandered from group to group of talking, dancing people, staring into their faces for a sign of her. And all the time I knew she was at Sophie's house, and even if she wanted to find us she wouldn't know where we were. I wanted her to play a game of Hideous kinky tag with me.

Mum and I discovered the ruins of a forgotten village. We went there most days to eat our lunch and trace our way through the mosaic of streets and courtyards and the rooms of houses that had once been a Roman town. Wild freesias and clumps of silver grass grew between the stone foundations, and the scent of the flowers hung over the town in an aromatic haze. We lounged in the sun and looked over the town and out to sea.

Mum was making me sandals. The soles were cut from thick leather in the shape of my feet, and the leather was sewn on to rubber from the tyre of a car. Now she was stitching short strips to the sides of each shoe. One round loop for my toe and two more to hold my feet in.

I drew pictures of houses. The houses weren't houses that I had actually seen, they were houses from books. I copied from memory the house that Madeleine had lived in when she woke up in the night with appendicitis and the house that was a hospital where they took her for an operation. I drew the house that was a shop from which Charlie bought his first bar of chocolate and the very small and shabby house where his grandparents George and Georgina and Joe and Josephine slept in two double beds and never got up.

'When we go home, can we live in a house with a garden?'

'All right.' Mum was decorating my sandals with beads.

'Do you mean all right yes or all right maybe?

'I mean,' she said, rethreading her needle, 'all right hopefully.'

We put off going back to Algiers and the overly sympathetic clerk from the British consulate for as long as we could. We spent whole days in the Roman town and sometimes stayed on with pockets full of dates to watch the sun setting over the sea. No one else ever arrived at the Youth Hostel and our room with two beds began to feel like home.

One day Mum worked out that we had exactly enough

money to pay the sculptor and get a bus back to the city and not a dirham more. Regretfully we said goodbye to the caretaker, who was still as shy and quiet as on the first day and, it seemed, had never got used to sharing his house with strangers, and went back to Algiers.

To the relief of everyone, especially the clerk, our money had arrived. We paid our debts and caught a train to Marrakech.

I was a babble of questions. 'How long will it take to get there?' 'What's the first thing we'll do when we arrive?' 'Do you think Bea will be glad to see us?' and 'Will Bilal be back?'

Mum read her book. She was the only person I knew who could turn off their ears like shutting an eye. Sometimes I resorted to hitting her with my closed fist to get the answer to a question. Even that didn't always work.

The train stopped at its first station. Mum shifted restlessly as I besieged her with questions. 'Are we nearly there?' 'Will we stop at lots of stations?' 'When can I have something to eat?'

She stood up. The train was rumbling in its tracks and the trees on the other side of the platform were slipping slowly backwards. She grabbed my arm and, using our bag as a barricade, she pushed her way along the corridor, until through a blur of noise and panic we stood in the empty station and watched as our train thundered into the distance.

Mum didn't offer any explanation. I decided not to mention the fact that my new sandals were now travelling on alone to Marrakech, tucked under a recently vacated train seat. Mum led the way out of the station.

The town looked familiar even though I couldn't see why it should. It was only when we reached the iron gates opening on to the formal garden that I realized why we'd jumped from a moving train. We stood in the courtyard of the Zaouia and waited.

'I just want to apologize to the Sufi.' Mum was talking to me again. 'I want to say that I understand now that their decision was probably right.'

The same red-bearded man came out to meet us. He nodded and smiled and gestured for us to follow him. 'Allah akhbar,' he muttered as he rushed us down an outside corridor, through the open doors of which the sounds of children playing seeped into the stillness of the courtyard.

The holy man threw open a door and showed us into a roughly whitewashed room. 'You see we were expecting you,' he said and he left us alone to rest before dinner.

CHAPTER TWENTY-FIVE

The men were all in white and they knelt in a circle around Sheikh Bentounes, who lived with his family in the residential corridor two doors down from us. Sheikh Bentounes was a holy man. He was the head of the Zaouia and the leader of the Sufis. Mum kept a black-and-white photograph of him in our room.

The boys sat in the circle with the men and wore white skull caps like their fathers. Mum and I sat with the women in their everyday clothes. We sat in a separate group half shielded by a curtain and sometimes the women joined in the praying and sometimes they didn't. I seized on this opportunity of showing off my turban, and secretly longed to sit strictly in full white uniform and pray in a circle around the sheikh.

The prayers sounded a little like the singing of the builders in the garden at Sid Zouin. Sheikh Bentounes breathed in deeply through his nose, pushing his stomach out under his soft white robes and then letting his voice turn into a song as he controlled his exhaling breath for minutes on end. The men and boys that faced him joined in a chorus that rose to a violent crescendo and then sank to a sigh as row after row bent their heads to rest their faces on the ground, leaving a soft silence hanging in the air with no noise but the whisper of perspiration trickling down the walls.

The prayers lasted for a whole afternoon and by the evening the walls of the room were awash with water. It collected in gullies and soaked into the carpet. One by one the children at the back of the room curled up on the floor and fell asleep as the men's voices rose up and up like sounds of the distant sea.

Early on each day of prayer a sheep arrived and was tethered to a post in the courtyard. I preferred the sheep's uncomprehending gaze to that of the children of Sheikh Bentounes. The sheikh with the red beard didn't have any children. He spent the mornings tending his roses. Sheikh Sidi Muhammad of the red beard was my enemy. He had shouted at me on the first day when I climbed into the rose bed to sniff the scent of a giant yellow rose. Sheikh Sidi Muhammad had shouted and waved his arms and rushed over to me and pulled me out of his garden by one ear. I tried to explain about smelling the flowers not picking them, but he interpreted the tears that sprang to my eyes as a sign of guilt and now he kept a stern watch over me at all times.

I confided in my sheep that he must be a very stupid man not to understand the difference between smelling and picking. Mum defended him. She said he lived in a state of extended spiritual ecstasy and that when he came down to earth it often made things rather difficult.

Everyone who had attended prayers was invited to eat at the Zaouia. That morning's sheep turned on a spit in the outside kitchen and the smell of the roasting meat drifted through the mosque in a haze of herbs and mouth-watering temptation.

'Are we going to stay here for ever?' I asked Mum, as, dazed and still half asleep, I waited for my kebab.

But Mum only said, 'As long as we need to,' and went to talk with Selina.

Selina was a lady who had been living at the Zaouia for years and years. Selina was sixty. Before she was a Sufi she had been a magician's assistant. I liked her better than anyone else even though she refused to show me any tricks. She said she couldn't remember tricks now she was a Sufi and even though I thought she was beautiful with her white hair and almond eyes, whenever Mum talked to her it made me worry and I thought of Bea and how she must think we had forgotten her.

Whether it was Selina's magic's fault or not, we stayed at the Zaouia – and the longer we stayed the more I hated it. Not because of the mosque, or the days themselves, which were a calm round of courtyards and prayers and whispering corridors, but because of the nights. Because of the Black Hand. I was convinced the disembodied hand was only waiting for its moment to close its sooty fingers round my throat. I lay awake against the warmth of Mum's sleeping body and waited for the slow thud of its approach. With every night's reprieve my anxiety did not lessen, but a new fear, a wild and uncontrollable fear, took hold of me. The Black Hand was going to strangle Mum.

Now I stayed awake at night with all the vigilance of a bodyguard, and when I could hardly bear to breathe in case I missed a noise, a clue, the thud of a thumb, I lifted my trembling hands and held them gently round her neck, lacing my fingers together so that not a chink of flesh was exposed. If Mum were strangled, my thoughts whirred in the stillness of our white room, I would be stranded for ever at the Zaouia. I saw Bea sitting at a window in Sophie's house hating us both for forgetting her and never knowing that I was trying to escape over the wrought-iron gate with the red-bearded sheikh close and grasping at my ankles.

I woke every morning, clammy and damp in a tangle of sodden sheet, but always in time to remove my fingers from around Mum's neck, the threat of the Black Hand seemingly insubstantial beside the misery of yet another ruined mattress. Mum didn't speak about my accidents but began wrapping our mattress in a plastic sheet that creaked and crackled as I lay in wait for the inevitable murder to be carried out.

Soon our white sheet, hand-washed by Mum, was a daily, dismal reminder of the night before, flapping dry on its line in the courtyard. I was sure I could detect a smirk of satisfaction on the face of Sidi Muhammad as he glanced from me to it, as though a punishment dreamt up by him were being carried out. I decided that if the worst came to the worst, I would run away and join a circus. Joining a circus would mean learning a trick. A new trick. Or any trick. I leant against the waxy wool of that day's sheep and dreamt.

I saw myself trumpeted into the ring in silver sequinned tights, heralded as the youngest ever walker of the tight-rope. The lions in their cages growled in suspense and the crowd gasped while I, high above them, shimmied across the roof of the circus tent on a hairline wire.

I would have to practise. I glanced over at the washing line. It drooped, wall to wall with drying clothes.

I could learn to juggle. I thought of my frustrated efforts in the garden at the Mellah as I tried to catch the bruised and sagging orange as it plummeted from one hand to the floor. Bilal had been encouraging at first, but as the days went by and the heap of squashed and abandoned oranges piled up in the garden he remained silent.

I decided I would teach myself to walk on my hands.

I began training that afternoon in a deserted yard behind the outside kitchen. It was where the sheep was dragged, its hind legs rigid in resistance, to have its throat cut with one slash of a knife.

'Hup, hup, hup,' I yelled, raising my arms for a flying dive as I raced across the yard, but at the last moment, as my hands touched down, my legs, which had been ready to soar into the air, lost confidence. They clung to my body at a pathetic angle, so that the flying leap that was to result in a handstand ended in yet another head-over-heels.

I lay on the ground and stared up at the sky. I thought about balancing acts on Bilal's shoulders and the well at the Barage where I had learnt to somersault from such a height. I dreamt about the acrobats that performed like red and green lizards in the square in Marrakech and how happy I would be if only I'd been born into their family. I lay in the sun and thought about the people who believed me when I told them I remembered my last life and how it had been lived out as an angel. I wondered if them believing me meant it could be true. I made a decision. I would start sleeping in the afternoons. If I slept in the afternoons I could stay awake at night. Then not only would I be on guard at the moment when the Black Hand rattled the handle of our door, but I would have a way of proving to Mum that I was too old to need a plastic sheet.

My plan seemed to me a great success. That first night I was convinced I had stayed awake till morning and even congratulated myself on getting up to pee in the bucket by the door. But even though I felt the shiver of the cold metal on my flesh, and remembered distinctly the sound of water drumming, I caught myself off guard, waking up to find it had only been a dream. There was the warm and familiar smell of my nightie sticking damply to me, and the bucket was empty.

'I think it would be nice to get home in time for Bea's birthday,' Mum said one day as we waited for prayers to begin. I had curled up on the floor of the mosque for my regular afternoon sleep. 'Would you like that?'

I was so excited I couldn't answer.

Bea's birthday meant that very soon it would be my birthday. Bea did everything first. It was useful because once Bea had done it I always knew what to expect. That was what was wrong with the Zaouia. Bea hadn't done it first. Or ever. If Bea were here, sleeping on a mattress on the other side of the room, maybe the Black Hand would turn itself back into a horror story in John's voice, loud and pretending to be scary.

Last year on my birthday we went on a picnic to the woods outside Marrakech in a horse-drawn taxi. Bilal had been there and Linda and Mob. Mum had given me a wooden box with leaves carved on it. I wondered what had happened to it. I leant against the damp wall of the mosque, perspiration dripping into my turban, and tried to remember what we had done last year on Bea's birthday. I knew it had been a surprise and, after two weeks of waiting, mine, even with the horse-drawn taxi, was a disappointment.

CHAPTER TWENTY-SIX

Mum and I boarded the same train for Marrakech we'd jumped from all those weeks before. Selina came to the station to see us off. I watched her hopefully as our train gathered speed, convinced that at the last moment she would relent and let fly at least one white dove from the sleeve of her djellaba.

It was early evening when we arrived in Marrakech and we went straight to Sophie's house to collect Bea. The house was shuttered and dark and there was no sign of anyone at home. Mum said they had probably all gone out for supper and if they weren't in the Djemaa El Fna someone would be sure to know where to find them.

They weren't in the Djemaa El Fna. Even the Fool, who wiped tears from his eyes as he sat at our table, didn't seem to have ever heard of Sophie. Bea, he was sure he had seen, but he couldn't remember when. Mum ordered two bowls of bissara, but by the time it came a hard lump had risen up in my throat making it difficult to swallow, and with the first scalding spoonful I stripped the skin from the roof of my mouth. I kept thinking Mum must know where Bea was. Maybe she was keeping it a secret so that it would be a surprise when we found her, but late that night when we arrived at Luna and Umbark's, it was Luna who was surprised.

'I was beginning to think you'd emigrated,' she said. Umbark was not at home.

Mum apologized. 'It's just that we've tried Sophie's house three times now and there's no one at home.'

Luna looked puzzled. 'They moved,' she said. 'Not long after you went away. He decided he needed the countryside to write.'

'Whereabouts in the countryside?' There was panic in Mum's voice.

'I'm not sure. I expect I could find out.' Luna was pouring tea. 'But Bea didn't go with them. In fact there was a bit of a scene.' Luna paused to concentrate as she raised the silver pot high like a Moroccan, cooling the tea in an arc before it settled in its cup. 'No. Bea wouldn't go,' she said admiringly. 'She refused to go. I think she was frightened that if she went away anywhere, you might not be able to find her when you came back.'

'Well, where is she then?'

'I would have had her here, but . . .' Luna glanced down at her stomach. It had ballooned under her clothes while we'd been gone. She looked around the room as if reminding herself how small it was. 'There's a man who lives in a communal house in the Medina . . . the man's name I don't know, but he has a dog, the dog is Mashipots.'

'And Bea went there?'

Luna had to restrain Mum from going to find her right then in the middle of the night. She made up a bed for us in the corner of the room and pretended not to notice when Mum took out the plastic sheet and slipped it under me.

We arrived at the communal house so early that we had to hammer on the door before even the dog began to bark. Finally a shutter clattered open and a man looked out.

'Bea? I've come to get Bea?' Mum shouted up.

The man frowned. 'Who?'

'Sophie? Are you a friend?'

'What?' The man rubbed his eyes.

'Do you have a dog called Mashipots?' Mum's voice was strained.

The man disappeared. We waited. Another shutter opened.

'What's Mashipots done now?' A new man leant out, naked.

'Is Mashipots your dog?'

'What if she is?'

'I'm Bea's mother.'

The man pulled back into the room and drew the shutters tight together. Eventually the door opened and a square-faced, white-and-tan dog flew out and jumped up to lick my face.

The man stood in the doorway. He was wrapped in a woman's dressing-gown. 'Bea's old lady, eh?' he said. 'Well, I'm sorry to disappoint you, man, but she's not here. Me an' Bea – we didn't quite see eye to eye.'

'What do you mean?'

'What I mean is that she ran off. Went out to buy a packet of cigarettes like, and, well, never came back.'

'Didn't you look for her?' Mum was pale. 'Down, Mashipots.' She kicked the dog who had its front paws on my shoulders.

'Easy, lady,' he said as Mashipots whimpered away. 'I didn't look for her because I thought if she wants to stay missionary-style with that old girl at the polio school, it's all the same to me.'

Mum didn't wait to hear any more. She tightened her grip on my hand and dragged me away.

There had been a party, and the trestle-tables were covered in half-eaten sandwiches and long pools of spilt lemonade. The room was full of children – boys with cropped hair, some even shaved, and mostly they had

163

sticks to help them walk. Mum and I stood in the doorway
and watched Bea coming towards us. She had grown taller
and wore a dress that I had never seen before. It was
checked a little like the tablecloths and had puffed sleeves.
She carried a plate of cake in her hand.

'Would you like some of my birthday cake?' she said
when she reached us and I took the plate and began to
cram the yellow sponge into my mouth.

'Happy birthday, darling,' Mum said and went to hug
her.

Bea stiffened. She pulled back and introduced Patricia.

Patricia was older than Mum and taller, and was
dressed very smartly with lace-up shoes. She watched as
I gobbled my cake.

'So you made it. Just in time,' she said, resting her hand
on Bea's shoulder. 'Come and join the party.'

Patricia took a plate and loaded it with sandwiches and
fruit and biscuits from the table and handed it to me.

'It's my birthday soon,' I told her.

'Really?' Her voice was cold and she walked away to
lift a boy off the floor who was dragging himself away
from the table, using his hands and nothing else.

Bea was on Patricia's side. They sat together over
English tea with milk and sugar and talked about their
own private things. They talked as if they had known each
other for ever.

'Why did you run away from Peter's?' Mum asked.
Peter was the owner of Mashipots.

Bea looked at her as if it were obvious. 'He made me
do hours and hours of maths homework and when I
wanted to go to the toilet he said I could only go if I called
it "the shithouse".'

I started to giggle.

'But I bet you've never had a birthday party like this
before,' Patricia said consolingly.

Bea shook her head. 'Never.' And she fixed Mum with

164

her Malteser eyes that were rounder than anyone else's.

'Me, neither,' I said. I wanted to be on Patricia's side too and have a birthday party like never before.

I asked Mum why Patricia didn't like me.

'Don't worry,' she said, 'she can't stand me, either.'

In the middle of that night, when I crawled into her bed to avoid the chill of my wet sheet, she whispered, 'We'll leave before she finds out,' and then added with a shiver, 'she reminds me of my mother.'

Patricia thought of all the polio boys as her children. She was very strict and dressed them in spotless white. She kept their hair so short it bristled. Bea talked to the boys and played with them, complicated games with pebbles and sticks that had to be caught and counted on the back of your hand. I tried to join in, but I was frightened by their twisted and emaciated legs and the boniness of their skulls with so little hair to hide behind.

Bea and I waited at the polio school while Mum looked for somewhere else to live. Patricia had objected to us going because it would mean missing lunch.

I sat with Bea on the steps of her dormitory. 'Don't you want to come and sleep in our room with us?' I asked her.

'No, I like it here,' she said. 'It's like being at boarding-school.'

'Have you ever been at boarding-school?'

'No, stupid.'

I was losing track of what Bea had and hadn't done.

'Do you like Patricia better than Mum then?'

'Maybe.'

'Mum'll be very unhappy.'

'Really?' she sounded like Patricia, and she skimmed a stone hard across the concrete.

I tried to think of something else to say. Everything in my head was jumbled and arguing. Bea continued to throw stones that were pieces of concrete that had come loose from the base of the step and I looked at my feet and wondered if I should tell her about the sandals that I left on the train.

'So tomorrow we'll move back to the Hotel Moulay Idriss,' Mum announced. She sat down on the step between us and took a packet out of her bag. She handed it to Bea. 'Happy birthday.'

Bea unwrapped her present slowly. Inside was a necklace of black and orange beads. Bea lifted up her hair for it to be fastened. It fitted tightly round her neck. She smiled a small smile in spite of herself.

That night Patricia and Mum had an argument. It started after supper when Bea spilt coffee on her checked dress. Patricia said it was ridiculous that a child of her age should be allowed to drink coffee just because she liked it, and then she put her arm around Bea and called her 'my little orphan'. Mum's eyes blazed and she cracked her plate down on the table so that it splintered. Patricia stood up. She insisted if they were going to argue they move into another room. The polio boys were taken off to bed, and Bea and I hovered as near to the closed door as we dared.

'What's she saying?' I whispered.

'Who?'

'Mum.'

'I don't know,' and Bea tapped me on the shoulder and hissed a murderous 'Mashipots' into my ear as she danced off down the row of tables.

CHAPTER TWENTY-SEVEN

'Akari said he saw Bilal. He was in a crowd at the Gnaoua.' We were walking through the narrow and familiar streets that led towards Nappy House.

'Bilal, Bilal, Mashipots and Mob,' I sang as we trudged along in the dark. Bea and I dragged the tartan duffle bag between us. 'Polio, powow, Zaouia and shithouse.' I was composing a new song especially for Bilal. 'Trampolining, fire-eating, central heating, shithouse.'

Moulay Idriss showed us to our old room and even donated two candles to unpack by and to light our way back and forth from our room to the toilet on the landing.

Mum read aloud a whole chapter of *Monkey* before she tucked us in. The Black Hand will never find us here, I thought as I lay on my mattress with Bea breathing softly by the other wall and Mum reading on by candlelight as she always did.

When I woke in the blackness of the shuttered room to find my bed still dry, I fumbled my way across to Mum's mattress to tell her the good news and to crawl in against the shininess of her nightdress, but as I edged my way under the covers I nudged up against the hard limbs of another body. A man. My face crimson I crept silently back to my own bed.

When I woke in the morning, Bilal was lighting the mijmar as if he had never been away. I leapt up with a

Red Indian war cry and threw myself at him. He stood and spun me round so fast I thought I would faint.

'There was a strange man in Mum's bed last night,' I told him when I had recovered my breath, but he just tickled the soles of my feet until tears rolled down my face and I begged and pleaded with him to stop.

Bilal was my Dad. No one denied it when I said so.

'Did you really used to know Luigi Mancini,' I asked him, 'when you wore silver and gold waistcoats?'

Bilal didn't think so. He didn't remember. He was working on a plan to make money out of my songs.

We went to the square to do research. 'Maybe Mum could sit inside a tent and tell people's fortune while I sing behind a curtain,' I suggested.

'And what would she tell them about their fortune?'

'She could find out from her *I Ching* book. Or maybe she could go to people's houses and heal the sick,' I said, remembering Ahmed's aunt in the mountains. 'And then I wouldn't have to sing at all.'

'Maybe. Maybe. Maybe.' Bilal set me down in front of our favourite acrobats as if to remind me that in his country children also have to work for a living.

Khadija came and squatted beside me. Her thin cotton caftan was ripped right along a seam and it made me think how in all the time I'd known her I'd never seen her in any other clothes. She rested her solemn face on her knees and watched the show. I wanted to give her something. I almost cried at the thought of the lost amethyst. If I'd only been able to carry some home I could have given her a splinter of purple glass to hang on the empty loops of plastic thread she wore as earrings. Even the drummer girls had beads.

On the morning of my birthday I was taken to the Henna Ladies to have my ears pierced. It was what I had asked for. 'Really it won't hurt a bit,' Mum assured me as we walked along the terrace. 'Just think of all those babies with little gold studs in their ears.'

'Will I have little gold studs?'

Mum paused. 'One day you will.'

The Henna Ladies sat me down on a mound of cushions. One of them began to thread a needle. The needle was a particularly fat needle, and knotted to the length of plastic thread that hung from its eye were three orange beads. I sat on my cushion and waited. I was expecting some kind of miracle so that I wouldn't be scared. I watched the point of the needle as it came towards me. The nearer it got, the further into the cushions I sank. The Henna Lady reached down and took hold of my ear and as the cold flat point of the metal pressed against my skin I began to scream.

'My God. What a fuss,' Mum said when we were safely back in our room.

'Maybe on my next birthday,' I said doubtfully.

Even if I'd gone through with the ear-piercing I still wouldn't have had anything to give Khadija. Three orange beads – I was scornful – and the promise of a gold stud.

It was the day after my birthday that Bea's lips went blue. She came home from school looking as if she'd been blackberry-picking.

Mum inspected the inside of her mouth. 'Does it hurt?'

'Of course it hurts.'

When Bea was ill there was nothing you could say. She had a way of turning things around and making you feel stupid.

'I have a mouth infection,' she said.

All Bea could eat was soup. Cold soup. Bilal suggested taking her to Umbark and the Gnaoua to see what they could do, but Bea refused point-blank. She sat with her hand over her mouth and scowled indignantly at us as we scooped up grains of couscous with our fingers and attempted to swallow them without appearing to chew.

That night when we were in bed Bea told me that if she closed her eyes and imagined biting down on a piece of toast she felt as if she were going to be sick. I'd never been sick. I asked her to show me how it was done. Bea turned towards the wall with one glum sweep of her blanket and refused to speak to me again.

Soon Bea's mouth had swelled up like a bluebottle. The bluer her lips became the whiter her face. Mum took her to see Aunty Rose. Mum had never met Aunty Rose, but she said she sounded like the kind of person who might know what to do.

Aunty Rose looked at Bea's lips and inspected the inside of her mouth. 'She has a gum infection.'

'You see,' Bea narrowed her eyes.

'All I can suggest is that you gargle with hot salt water. I don't expect you have any medical insurance?'

Mum said she didn't.

Aunty Rose made me open my mouth too. She tutted and put one finger right in. 'Thank heavens they're only your baby set,' she said.

Aunty Rose boiled a kettle and showed Bea how to gargle. 'Ow, ow, ow,' Bea moaned between mouthfuls of salt water.

'If I were you, my dear' – Aunty Rose looked at Mum as if she were a child – 'I'd think about getting home.' She said 'home' in a certain way that made me know she wasn't talking about the Hotel Moulay Idriss. 'I'll pray for you,' she said as we left.

Aunty Rose was a Christian. She had been living in Morocco for twenty years and she had one convert. Mum didn't like her much. She didn't say so, but she was quiet on the way home. We walked single file, Bea with her hand over her mouth in case she saw anyone from school, and me furious that I hadn't had a chance to mention my birthday.

Mum boiled water over the mijmar and Bea stayed home from school to gargle and spit into a bucket. Bilal brought her goat's yoghurt and figs from the market and I offered to give up one of my dolls. Bea wasn't interested in dolls. She lay on the mattress in the darkest corner of the room and made me tell her stories. I told a story about Aladdin and his friend Bea the Bad who overheard Aladdin mumbling 'Open Sesame' in his sleep. Bea the Bad used the magic password to open the stone walls of the secret cave and steal all the treasure. Bea the Bad became Bea the Beautiful and moved into a palace next door to Luigi Mancini where they lived happily ever after.

When I finished the story she said, 'Just one more. Go on. I'll owe you.' She never even minded if I told her the same story twice.

On the day Mum took Bea to the doctor she owed me twenty-two stories. I waited at home with Bilal. We sat in the courtyard under the banana tree and Bilal smoked and I watched the Henna Ladies talking to their men on the upstairs landing. One of them was wearing Mum's stolen trousers under her caftan. I could see the pink velvet bell-bottoms flapping when she walked.

Bilal was still racking his brains for a plan to make some money. He scratched little patterns in the dust and when Moulay Idriss crossed the courtyard he didn't lift his eyes to greet him but hissed, 'Don't stare or he'll start asking for his rent.'

When Bea came home from the doctor, she went straight upstairs and lay down on her bed. I stood in the doorway.

'Did he give you any medicine?'

At first she didn't say anything but then, when I went on standing there shuffling my feet, she mumbled furiously, 'If you really want to know, my teeth are going to fall out.'

'All of them?'

Mum was very worried. She made Bea take the different pills the doctor had prescribed and stayed in with her all day. She rubbed cream from a tube on to her mouth. Bea lay still and waited. Whenever she woke, she stared hard at her pillow as if she expected to see it scattered with little lumps of tooth. For a week we waited for them to drop out. Mum even promised that as soon as we had enough money we would go back to England where you could get a false set on the National Health.

Bilal and I spent our days wandering through the market looking for soft things for Bea to eat. Sometimes the Fool came too. I studied him carefully at mealtimes, hoping to pick up some useful tips. But there was a difference: the Fool had one tooth, whereas Bea's doctor had said 'All'. The Fool just spiked his food and swallowed.

One day I looked at Bea and realized that her lips were no longer blue. I had been waiting so patiently for her teeth to drop out that I hadn't noticed she was getting better. I tried to hide my disappointment. I liked having Bea at home and even though I made a show of protest, being bullied into telling her stories was in fact my favourite pastime.

CHAPTER TWENTY-EIGHT

Bilal wanted us to leave the Hotel. Secretly. At night. He said he would show us the ancient city of Fes and take us to the beach at Agadir. Mum wouldn't agree. 'We've hardly got enough money for food,' she said, 'and anyway Moulay Idriss is our friend.'

That was when Bilal hit upon his plan. It was the plan he had been searching for in his head since before my birthday. Bilal demanded a pen and a piece of paper. He rested the paper against a book and began to write. He wrote slowly and carefully.

'What does it say?' I leant across his back. The writing closely resembled the black squiggles in Bea's schoolbook. She tried to make it out, but couldn't.

Bilal wrote until he reached the bottom of the page and then he handed back Mum's pen. He stood up and read his letter like a proclamation. The letter was in Arabic. Bea creased up her eyes and listened.

'It's begging,' Bea said when he had finished, and she turned her back and walked out on to the landing.

'There are five pillars that every good Muslim must stand by,' Bilal explained. 'He must say his prayers. Study the Koran. Fast. Go to Mecca once in his life if he possibly can. And give alms to the poor and hospitality to strangers.'

Mum listened. She wasn't angry like Bea, but she wasn't

sure. If Mum wasn't sure, there was nothing Bilal could do. He rolled the letter into a scroll and tied it with a ribbon. He set it neatly in the corner of the room.

The days were not so hot as they had been and sometimes it even rained. I kept wondering if we'd missed Christmas. Bea and I decided to visit Aunty Rose to see if her clay figures were out on display. No one answered the door when we knocked. We peered through the windows. The furniture was covered in white sheets and Mary, Joseph and the cradle were nowhere to be seen. We waited patiently for her to reappear, but when it began to grow dark and there was still no sign, we gave up and headed for home.

I was walking a little behind Bea, re-examining in my mind the great injustice of Aunty Rose and the pyjamas and how such a mistake could be overlooked. I was wearing my pyjamas now under my burnous, and even though I had grown taller in the last year the trouser legs still needed turning over twice. 'Hideous kinky,' I muttered and I felt for the rash on my arm to remind myself of left and right so I could begin a marching song with my feet. 'Left, left.' I scratched my arm. 'Left my wife and five fat children. Right, right.' There was no rash on my right arm. 'Right in the middle of the kitchen floor.' Bea stopped short ahead of me and I marched on into her. Her breath came in gasps through her nose and she put out her hand to hold me back.

Through the darkness between two buildings a man was reeling. He was bent over, staggering backwards and away from a figure that glimmered like steel and, as the man who was an old man thudded against a wall, his attacker lunged forward and struck him hard. His head cracked against the stone and he fell forward. As he fell his babouche slipped and twisted through the air, and then for no reason I knew it was the Fool. It was the Fool

174

and I had never thought before what an old and fragile man he was. Through the darkness that was no longer dim but clear and fine like silk I could see the strength of the other man, I saw his shoulders flex under his light djellaba and a swift, brown leg pull back. Bea gripped my arm and forced me on along the street. I wanted to run screaming into the fight and save the Fool and take him home, but as we dragged ourselves away, I saw his raised and clinging hand flutter to the ground and the beating of his limp and broken body rang in my ears. Bea let go of my hand and I raced after her up the staircase to the second landing. There was no one home. Bea lit a candle. A note lay just inside the door. 'Luna's baby has arrived. Be back later. Mum.'

Bea tore the note into tiny pieces and scattered them over the floor. Then she lay down on her bed. I went over to check on Mary, Mary-Rose and Rosemary. I remade their beds and smoothed their clothes and regretted that their hair was made of wool so that it frayed and frizzled if I brushed it.

I didn't say anything to anyone about the fight. I waited for Bea to mention it, or for someone to notice that the Fool no longer danced with the Gnaoua in the afternoons, or silently escorted us at night. Nothing was said. Occasionally I looked at Bea to see if she was running over those events like I was, the sound effects living their own life behind her eyes, but she gave nothing away.

It was raining a warm rain that slanted down in showers when Mum agreed to go along with Bilal's plan. Moulay Idriss had visited us in our room and it seemed there was no time to waste. First Bilal went to check his letter with Abu Kier. Abu Kier was a man who was concerned with his spirit, Mum said. People understood about Abu Kier. He sat in the market in his tattered djellaba and they gave him food and money. Abu Kier gave his blessing to Bilal's letter.

Now Mum was in a hurry. She draped my burnous over my shoulders and buttoned its one cloth button at my neck. My burnous was camel-coloured. Bea's was made from darker, thicker wool like the coat of a donkey, and Mum's was white. We stood in the street with our hoods around our ears while Mum kept the letter under her cloak to stop it from getting wet. Bilal wasn't coming with us. When I asked him why, he explained that it wasn't part of the plan.

Bea and I followed Mum towards the Djemaa El Fna. She held us each by the hand and walked fast, heading for the shops that surrounded the square. We passed Khadija, Zara and Saida talking to the waterman, but Bea pretended not to see that it was them and, as I turned to call out, Mum tugged my hand to keep me from falling behind.

We stopped by a shop that sold carpets. The sun struck out from behind a cloud and splintered through the rain in a dazzling shower of gold. She held the letter out in front of her so that the carpet merchant would know why we were there and wouldn't try and sell us any carpets. He took the letter. He had a kind face and he lifted me up on to a tottering mountain of prayer mats before he read it. He read carefully and nodded while he did so. Mum had told me what it said: 'In the name of God I am a stranger in your town, fallen on a hard moment . . .'

Bea's face was blank. 'Hideous,' I whispered at her but she wasn't playing.

The carpet man handed the letter back to Mum and without a word took some coins from a box at the back of his shop and presented them to her.

'I'm hungry,' I said once we were outside. We had left home before the mijmar was alight and I couldn't remember having had any breakfast.

Mum hurried on towards a shop which sold things

176

made from brass – weighing-scales and pots and pipes in different shapes and sizes. There were two men smoking inside the shop. They looked like brothers. Mum took a deep breath before she entered. Once the brothers had read the letter, each in turn, they insisted we sit down and they called to a woman to bring us mint tea. Bea shrugged her shoulders at me and asked for a second cup. The men in the brass shop were very generous. They gave Mum a handful of dirhams, which she put with the others in her purse.

We only visited the larger shops that sold carpets or boxes and bags made from leather, and the more money Mum collected the more courageous she became. As we moved through the streets between the shops, she held the letter out in front of her for everyone to see.

Bea and I kept our eyes on the ground.

People stopped. They glanced at the letter and stared at us, but before they moved away they always added at least a centime to our collection.

The only person who questioned us was an American. He scrutinized the letter. Who was Mum? Where was she from? Why didn't she have any money? He said he wanted to help us, but until he was utterly convinced by our story he didn't feel he could. At first Mum tried to answer his questions. Then she became irritable. 'You are inter-rupting my begging time,' she said. 'Can't you see I'm working?' And she took Bea and me by the hand and moved away.

We worked all day. We moved around the square, traipsing in and out of shops and standing in the street to stop the people who were coming from the market. We never even paused to talk or drink coffee with our friends. Once I saw Abu Kier watching us from the corner of the street. I tried to point him out to Mum, but in the moment that I looked away he'd vanished. As the day wore on I didn't mind so much about the letter and the fact that we were begging, and from time to time even Bea forgot and lifted her eyes from the ground.

Mum's purse was full. It rattled when she walked. She rolled the letter back into its scroll and tucked it inside her burnous.

'That is a once in a life-time kind of thing,' she said, to my relief.

CHAPTER TWENTY-NINE

Moulay Idriss was waiting patiently. He watched us as we trudged up the corner stairs. Mum tipped the money out on to the floor and Bilal began to count. He heaped the coins into separate piles, arranging them into towers of various size and colour. When every coin was in formation, Bilal jumped up and called Moulay Idriss in to take away his rent. He put his arms around Mum and held her close.

'Bilal, Bilal,' I said after more than a minute. I had crawled across the floor and was hanging on to his leg. 'What are we going to do with the rest of the money?'

Bilal let go of Mum. He picked me up by my feet and dangled me upside down. I could see four towers of coins swimming.

'I'm hungry,' I said between gulps of laughter. 'And Bea wants a Mars Bar.' Bilal didn't know what a Mars Bar was. 'When we go to England,' I said, 'I'll buy you one with my pocket money.'

It was some time since we had eaten in the square and we ordered meat kebabs and snails and bowls of oily spinach. 'If our money ever does come through,' Mum said, once we had started to eat, 'maybe we really should think about getting home.'

She wasn't speaking to anyone in particular. Bea looked at her over a wedge of bread. She didn't say anything. Bilal eased a rubbery snail out of its shell. He didn't seem to have heard. Bea continued to chew thoughtfully and Mum stopped eating to smoke.

When the meal was over and our plates had been cleared away, Bea, without warning, sank her head on to her hands and burst into tears. I stared at her bobbing head. I couldn't remember ever having seen Bea cry. Bea didn't cry. It was me and Mum who cried.

'If we do go home,' she sobbed into the table, 'does it mean we won't ever be able to come back?'

Mum put her arm around her. She stroked her despairing head. 'If you look up at the sky,' she told her, 'you can see seven stars that make a pattern.' Bea raised her head and I followed her gaze. The sky dripped with stars, they hung in a mist behind the orange glow of the city. 'Those stars are the seven brothers of the seven prophets and whoever makes a wish to them, it will come true.'

Bea lifted her head high, her tears already drying on her cheeks. 'Oh that's all right then,' she said, and she closed her eyes and with her face tilted up towards the seven stars she moved her lips silently in a long and complicated prayer.

'I think it would be nice to buy Khadija a present,' Mum suggested. It was the day our money had arrived at the bank.

'And Zara and Saida,' Bea added.

We found the three friends sitting in a circle around an empty bottle of Fanta. 'Waa, waa,' they called to us as we approached. Mum took Saida by the hand and led us around the edge of the Djemaa El Fna and into the covered market on the far side. We followed her down aisle after aisle of slippers and purses and gold belts until we came to the stall where I had bought my first caftan. I was wearing it now and the orange-and-raspberry pink of the cloth seemed hardly to have faded. Khadija, Saida and Zara looked up at the rows of dresses with longing eyes.

'Choose one,' Mum urged, and they looked at Bea and me for confirmation. 'Choose one. Choose one,' we insisted.

The man in the shop would not let them touch. They pointed and giggled and sighed over each dress as he held up one after the other for their inspection. Khadija chose a pale green dress with the crescent-shaped pattern of leaves embossed into the material. She wanted to put it on right then, but Mum insisted that it be wrapped in paper, and she carried it under her arm. Zara and Saida both chose dresses in thick, shiny nylon. One in blue and pink and the other in a swirling paisley of red and yellow. Mum held all three packages under her arm and we followed her on down the avenues of everything you ever dreamed of.

Mum wouldn't say where we were going. She walked fast through the old city and we followed her, all five dancing and skipping to keep up. She stopped at the doors of the Hammam. 'Have you been here before?' she asked them. They hadn't.

They peeled off their ragged dresses which was all they wore and Mum took a bottle of shampoo out of her bag. She stood them in a line and poured water over their heads. Bea and I showed them how you could stand your hair on end when it was thick with the lather of the shampoo so that you looked as if you had seen a ghost or you were a ghost. Mum rubbed us down with the Hammam stone and then she left us in a warm and steamy room to drip and chatter while she washed her own hair which was much too long and heavy to ever stand on end. When we were dry she combed our hair through with almond oil. Otherwise, she said, it would break the hair-brush. I wished we still had our tin of powder so that they could know how silky it felt between your toes but, when

Mum unpacked the caftans and dropped each one over their heads, Khadija, Zara and Saida looked at themselves with such wonder that nothing else mattered.

The following morning a woman tapped on our door. She had grey hair and a bent back. She was Khadija's mother. She thanked Mum over and over, and every time she thanked her a tear rolled down her cheek and over the top of her veil. After she had gone Mum cried too but she wouldn't say why.

We went to visit Akari in his shop and Bilal came with us and carried Mum's sewing-machine as a present for Akari's wife. Akari tried to convince us to stay. He said he had a house we could rent in the French quarter. We could live there free if Mum were to sew an English dress every month for his little girls. He said he would even take us to another camel festival.

I didn't like to think about the camel festival. The camel, garlanded in flowers, had collected us from our house in the Mellah, and we had followed it out of the city and high into the mountains in a procession of singing. We had walked for the whole day and only arrived in time to see the camel sinking to its knees, forcing itself up again, staggering, and all the time its severed head was bouncing and grazing down the mountainside. Bea said it hadn't rolled down the mountain at all, and that she had seen the camel's head with her own eyes being packed into a straw basket. Mum had lagged behind with Akari and only arrived at the top in time to eat a slice of camel cheese and negotiate a donkey ride for the journey down.

We said goodbye to Luna and Umbark and their tiny baby. Luna was so happy that even though she was sad when she said goodbye I could still see her smiling underneath. We packed all our things into the tartan duffle bag and what was left over into a sack Mum had made out of a bedspread. I left my black trousers out to wear on the journey.

'When you are too big for your trousers,' Bilal said to me, 'I want you to take off my patch and sew it on to something else.' He made me promise. That was when I knew he wasn't coming with us.

CHAPTER THIRTY

The streets of Marrakech were lined with people on the morning that we said goodbye to the Nappy Ladies and Ayesha and her grandmother and Moulay Idriss and made our way to the train station. There were rows of flags strung up above the crowd, and in the distance short, sharp volleys of gunfire rang out. Bilal carried our bags. He edged his way through the people who streamed down the avenues of orange trees towards the gates of the city and I held tightly on to the tail of his djellaba so as not to be swept away. 'We're going to miss our train,' Mum shouted over my head.

I saw Khadija standing in a wall of people holding a flag. She ran out to us.

'What's going on?' Bea shouted to her.

'It's the birthday of the King.' And she waved her flag and danced.

Then I noticed Khadija's dress. She was wearing her old caftan, torn and filthy with the rip that went up above her knees.

'What happened to your new dress?' Mum bent down to her.

Khadija darted away into the crowd. We pressed ourselves against the wall of people and waited for her, but she didn't come back.

A crack like thunder shook the air. The street where

we stood cleared as if by magic and the people pressed themselves back against the buildings and craned their necks to see. Bilal lifted me on to his shoulders. A group of men with guns marched into view. They were followed by an army of horses that trotted and scampered, their tails arched and their heads held high. Their riders wore swords that curved down from their belts, and their clothes were trimmed with braid. I could feel the hearts of a thousand people stopping and starting. And then an open carriage rolled into view. It was drawn by four black horses. Inside sat the King of Morocco. The voice of the crowd burst out in a frenzy of delight. They shouted and strained and waved their arms at him, and in return the King stood up in his carriage and put his hand over his heart.

We streamed after the King's carriage. We were squeezed through the gate of the city and emerged on the plain where once we had tried to sell Mary, Mary-Rose and Rosemary. As the King's carriage rolled through the gates, a line of Berber horsemen, who had been waiting in a silent salute, raised their guns and at sudden speed charged the carriage. The city froze as the horses thundered down on the King. Until with a simultaneous ringing shot of their rifles they skidded to a halt. I watched spellbound from Bilal's shoulders. The men charged and the Berber women danced. They accompanied themselves with a noise like a Red Indian whoop that made me laugh. It ended on a short shriek like a marsh bird.

'We've missed our train, surely,' Mum called, and we began to extricate ourselves from the crowd, to squeeze and shoulder our way back through the hustle of the celebrations to find a taxi that was not on holiday.

Our train was waiting. Bilal got on with us and found a place where we could sit beside a window. He packed our bags into the racks above the seat. I was wrong. He is coming with us, I thought, and as I thought it, Bilal was walking backwards, smiling with his smiling eyes until, without a word, he had disappeared among the last-minute passengers. Bea and I searched the length of the train and hung out of every window, willing him to reappear.

'Bilal! Bilal!' we shouted as the train began to pull away. 'Bilal!' But I couldn't pick him out among the crowd dispersing on the platform.

The train rumbled down a track banked with the first flowers of spring, with wild hollyhocks and tiny clinging roses, and entered the gloom of an avenue of eucalyptus trees. Marrakech stretched behind us in the distance.

'Does this train go all the way home?' I asked Mum, who was braiding and unbraiding her hair with quick, distracted fingers.

'No,' she said. I had to pinch her for the answer.

Bea had climbed up into an empty luggage rack and was using it as a hammock. 'Hideous, hideous, hideous kinky, hideous, hideous kink,' she chanted softly to the rhythm of the wheels.

I badly wanted to climb up and join her, but I thought it would be safest to stay on the seat in case Mum changed her mind about going home and decided at the last minute to jump off at one of the stations along the way.